Cipher of Sanity

Unraveling the Shadows of Veridian

Victoria S. Grant

Table of Contents

Chapter 1
The Bizarre Murder

As night descended on the gothic sprawl of Veridian City, a relentless downpour had transformed the streets into rivulets of shimmering silver under the feeble glow of street lamps. Amidst this dreary backdrop, Detective Leo Marquez's cruiser cut through the mist, the wipers working tirelessly against the onslaught of rain. Beside him, Dr. Elise Bennett, her features bathed in the ghostly light of the dashboard, appeared lost in thought, her eyes reflecting a storm more tumultuous than the one battering the city.

The car pulled into an alley shadowed between towering old buildings, their stone facades weeping with rain. Leo parked near the police tape that flickered in the wind like a spectral barrier. They stepped out, their boots splashing in puddles that mirrored the tumultuous sky above.

"The body's this way," said Officer Dale, who approached them with an umbrella that barely held off the rain. They followed him under the skeletal arms of fire escapes dripping with precipitation, to where the crime scene awaited.

The victim was a male, late forties, sprawled face-up on the cobblestones. His chest was bare despite the chill, carved with symbols that looked ancient and arcane—cruel, precise cuts that turned his torso into a grotesque canvas. A police photographer's flash sporadically illuminated the scene, capturing each detail with stark clarity.

Elise knelt beside the body, her professional calm juxtaposing the gruesome spectacle. She traced the air above the carvings with a pale finger, careful not to disturb the mortal testament. "These are no random cuts," she murmured, more to herself than to Leo. "They're symbols... esoteric, possibly ritualistic."

Leo, who had been conversing with another officer, turned his attention to her. "Symbols? What, like some cult stuff?"

"Possibly," Elise replied, her gaze still fixed on the markings. "I need to research these... they look familiar, like something out of the psychological texts from the early 20th century."

The detective frowned, his pragmatic mind grappling with the abstract. "Let's keep it grounded, Bennett. We've got a dead psychologist, carved up in an alley—"

"He was a psychologist?" Elise interrupted, her interest piqued as she stood to face Leo. The rain had plastered her hair to her face, giving her an almost spectral visage.

"Yeah, Dr. Harold Greaves. Specialized in neurotic disorders and experimental therapies." Leo handed her a plastic-covered document, a photo of the victim smiling at a conference. "He was pretty well-known in his field."

Elise's mind raced, connecting dots that seemed increasingly disturbing. "Experimental, you say? That might explain the symbols... They could be a message or a signature."

Leo looked skeptical but nodded, knowing better than to dismiss her instincts outright. "We'll canvass the area, see if anyone saw anything unusual. But this rain..." His voice trailed off as he glanced up at the relentless downpour, doubting any witness would have lingered in such weather.

As they wrapped up at the scene, Elise's phone buzzed. She glanced at the screen—a message from the forensic team. They had found something else at the victim's office. A book, old and possibly rare, hidden in a false bottom drawer.

Elise showed the message to Leo, her eyes alight with a mixture of dread and excitement. "This could be the key to understanding the symbols."

Leo's expression hardened with resolve. "Let's go check it out. We've got a killer to catch, and it looks like you just found our first real lead."

The rain continued to pour as they made their way back to the car, the night young and full of secrets yet to be uncovered. The city, with its gothic shadows and ancient whispers, seemed to watch them leave, the very air charged with the weight of impending revelations.

Under the harsh glare of fluorescent lights at the precinct, the atmosphere was tense as Detective Leo Marquez and Dr. Elise Bennett pored over the items collected from Dr. Harold Greaves' office. The room was cluttered with evidence bags, each meticulously labeled, but it was the ancient book Elise had mentioned earlier that dominated their focus. The text, bound in worn leather and adorned with intricate, faded gold leaf, lay open on a large examination table.

"Can you make anything out of this?" Leo asked, his tone a mix of skepticism and curiosity as he gestured towards the arcane symbols that peppered the pages.

Elise, her eyes scanning the cryptic text, responded without looking up. "Some of these symbols are astrological, others are more obscure. This text is not just rare; it might be one of a kind. It's a compendium of psychological and alchemical knowledge that seems eerily aligned with the markings on Dr. Greaves' body."

A detective, who had been reviewing security footage on a nearby screen, called out. "Detective Marquez, you need to see this." He paused the footage on a grainy image of a hooded figure entering the building where Dr. Greaves' office was located. The timestamp showed it was late at night, not long before the doctor was found dead.

Leo joined the detective, studying the figure. "Any luck on facial recognition?"

"Nothing yet. The hood obscures the face, and the camera angle doesn't help," the detective replied, frustration evident in his voice.

Back at the table, Elise carefully turned a page of the ancient book, her fingers trembling slightly under the weight of her discovery. "Leo, look at this," she called out, her voice a blend of excitement and concern.

Leo approached, his gaze following where Elise pointed. The page showed a detailed illustration of a human figure, the same symbols that were carved on Dr. Greaves' body surrounding it in a specific, ritualistic pattern.

"This is a ritual circle," Elise explained, her tone serious. "It's used in esoteric practices for... purification or rebirth. Whoever did this to Dr. Greaves might have believed they were performing a ritual."

"Or wanted us to think that," Leo added, his mind racing through the possibilities. "It's either a deranged killer with a penchant for the dramatic or someone trying to send a message."

The sound of footsteps approaching paused their discussion. Captain Emilio Sandoval entered the room, his expression grave. "How are we doing here?"

Elise responded before Leo could. "We may be dealing with a ritualistic killing, Captain. The symbols on Dr. Greaves' body are linked to ancient psychological and alchemical practices. We found them in this book, which was hidden in his office."

The captain rubbed his chin, processing the information. "Keep digging and see what else you can find out. I want hourly updates. This isn't just another murder; it's a statement."

As the captain left, Leo turned to Elise, a plan forming in his mind. "Let's get the lab to run a full analysis on the book and the symbols. Maybe they can find something we missed. In the meantime, I'll arrange to speak to

Dr. Greaves' colleagues and family. Someone must know something about his interests in these... practices."

Elise nodded, her mind already on the next steps. "I'll go through his research publications. There has to be a connection between his work and the symbols."

The precinct buzzed with the energy of active investigations, but in their corner of the station, the world seemed to narrow down to the mystery of the bizarre murder and its cryptic clues. Each piece of evidence added layers to the puzzle, each revelation a step closer to understanding the dark mind behind the crime.

As Leo organized the interviews, Elise continued her examination of the book. Her eyes were drawn to a margin note, written in a shaky hand that contrasted with the precise symbols. It was a single word, a name: "Puppeteer."

Chills ran down her spine as she muttered the name under her breath, unsure yet of its significance but feeling the weight of its ominous undertone. Leo, catching the tail end of her whisper, looked up, concern etching his features. "What did you find?"

"Puppeteer," Elise replied, the word hanging between them like a dark prophecy, their investigation deepening into the night, surrounded by the silent hum of fluorescent lights and the heavy promise of secrets yet to unfold.

Elise sat back in her chair, the leather creaking under her weight as she flipped through another one of Dr. Greaves' research papers. Across the desk, Leo was on the phone, his voice low but tense as he pressed the person on the other end for more information.

"Yes, any colleague, friend, anyone who knew about his personal interests or... yes, even hobbies that might seem out of the ordinary," Leo insisted, scribbling notes on a pad. He hung up with a frustrated sigh and looked over at Elise. "Nothing substantial. It's like nobody knew the guy beyond his work."

Elise glanced up from the papers, her expression thoughtful. "That might be the first clue, Leo. If he was involved in something secretive enough to require rituals, he wouldn't have broadcast it."

Leo leaned back, rubbing the bridge of his nose. "Secretive, right. Which brings us back to square one—why him? What made him the target for such a... spectacle?"

"There's a pattern in his work," Elise began, her voice carrying a mix of excitement and gravity as she spread several papers before them. "His later research, it shifted from standard psychological practices to more... esoteric theories. See here," she tapped a paragraph where Greaves discussed the psychological impact of ritualistic behaviors and ancient symbolism on modern therapy.

"Esoteric theories?" Leo raised an eyebrow, his skepticism palpable. "That's a leap from standard practice. Could have alienated him from the mainstream community."

"Exactly, and maybe that alienation is what drew him into whatever got him killed." Elise's fingers traced the lines of text, as if trying to absorb the hidden meanings through touch. "This might not have been mere interest; it could have been obsession."

The room was silent for a moment, save for the distant sounds of activity in the precinct. Leo broke the silence, his tone more contemplative. "An obsession that perhaps someone took advantage of? Or maybe he stumbled upon something he shouldn't have?"

"It's possible," Elise nodded slowly. "And there's this—'Puppeteer.' I found the name in the margin of his book. It's come up a few times in these papers too."

Leo perked up at that. "Puppeteer? That sounds more like a nickname than a scholarly reference. Could be our suspect, or maybe a co-conspirator?"

"I think we should consider the possibility that Dr. Greaves was part of a group," Elise suggested, her mind racing with the implications. "This 'Puppeteer' could be a key figure within it."

Leo stood, his decision made. "I'll put out feelers, see if this Puppeteer name pops up anywhere else—chat rooms, forums, anywhere someone with these... interests might hang out."

"And I'll dig deeper into the psychological significance of the symbols," Elise added, her gaze returning to the stack of research. "There has to be a connection between his theories and what was done to him."

As Leo prepared to leave the room, he paused at the door, looking back at Elise with a seriousness that matched the gravity of their case. "Be careful, Elise. We don't know what we're dealing with yet. This Puppeteer, if he's what we think, might not appreciate us digging around."

Elise met his gaze, her own steely and determined. "I can handle myself, Leo. Besides, we can't let this go. Greaves' death was a message. We need to find out what it was trying to say."

Leo nodded, the mutual understanding between them clear. He stepped out into the corridor, his steps echoing down the hall as he made his way to follow up on the new leads.

Left alone with her thoughts and the flickering light of her desk lamp, Elise turned her attention back to the papers. Each symbol, each reference to the Puppeteer, drew her deeper into a world that Dr. Greaves had perhaps been too entrenched in—one that might have led to his untimely demise. The shadows in the room seemed to creep closer as she delved further, the weight of the unknown pressing down upon her with each page turned.

The precinct's buzz had dwindled to the sporadic clacks of a keyboard and the distant murmur of late-night shift changes by the time Elise made another discovery. Her eyes, weary yet determined, caught a series of notes hidden in the margins of Dr. Greaves' research papers. These weren't just scribbles; they were dates and locations, cryptically noted yet clearly significant. She mapped them out, tracing lines between what seemed random, only to reveal a pattern that suggested meetings or events.

Elise was so engrossed in her findings that she almost didn't notice Leo returning to the office. He leaned against the doorframe, watching her for a moment before breaking the silence. "Anything new?"

She looked up, her face illuminated by the soft glow of the lamp. "Maybe. Look at this." She spread out a city map on the desk, dotted with the locations from Greaves' notes. "These aren't random. They correlate with the dates he was unusually absent from the university."

Leo stepped closer, studying the map. "Scheduled events?"

"Or secret meetings," Elise suggested. "And they're all in old parts of the city, near historical landmarks. It's consistent with someone obsessed with the past, rituals, and maybe..."

"The occult," Leo finished for her, his tone a mix of reluctance and realization.

"Yes," Elise nodded, her finger pausing over one location marked more frequently than others. "This one, in particular, shows up multiple times. It's an old church, deconsecrated and mostly abandoned now. A perfect place for... whatever they were doing."

Leo's expression hardened. "We should check it out."

"Tomorrow morning," Elise agreed, already gathering her things. "It's too late tonight, and we need to be prepared for what we might find."

They were about to leave when Elise's phone buzzed with a new email notification. She checked the message, her brow furrowing as she read. "It's from the university. Greaves' colleague finally responded. He's willing to talk about Greaves' research interests outside the university."

"That could help fill in some gaps," Leo noted, watching as Elise typed a quick reply.

"Yes, I'll meet him tomorrow after we check out the church." She locked her phone and slipped it into her bag, her mind already racing through the possibilities of what the next day would hold.

As they left the building, the night air felt unusually chill, a foreboding silence enveloping the city streets. They walked to the parking lot, their steps quick and purposeful, each lost in their thoughts about the case.

At their cars, Leo turned to Elise. "Be careful, okay? If we're right about this, we're stirring up something big."

Elise nodded, her features set in a grim determination. "I know. See you at the church at 8?"

"8 it is," Leo confirmed, watching her drive off into the night before getting into his own car.

As Elise drove through the deserted streets, the city's shadows seemed to watch her pass, the weight of the unknown growing heavier with each mile. The pieces were coming together, but the picture they formed was one of danger and dark secrets, hidden in the depths of Veridian's historical heart.

Meanwhile, Leo drove in the opposite direction, his mind replaying their findings, each detail a thread in a complex web they were only beginning to unravel. The church loomed in his thoughts, a beacon of mysteries yet to be uncovered.

And somewhere in the city, behind the facade of an ordinary building, a phone rang in a darkened room. The voice that answered was calm, measured, but carried an undercurrent of alarm. "They know about the church. Prepare for visitors."

The line went dead, the night reclaiming its silence, as the players on both sides readied for the confrontations to come.

Chapter 2
Cryptic Clues

The early morning light spilled through the blinds of the forensic lab, casting long shadows across the tables cluttered with evidence from Dr. Harold Greaves' office and the murder scene. Elise Bennett and Leo Marquez stood over a large table where the contents of Greaves' briefcase had been spread out, including the ancient book and several encrypted notes they had found tucked away.

Leo picked up one of the notes, examining the peculiar symbols scrawled across it. "Any luck making sense of this yet?"

Elise, who had been poring over a similar note, glanced up. "It's not standard encryption or any modern cipher. It looks more like it's based on historical alchemical symbols mixed with what might be a personal shorthand. We're dealing with someone who had a deep knowledge of ancient texts, possibly even occult practices."

"Great, a killer with a penchant for puzzles and the occult," Leo muttered, setting the note back down. "How do you even start to crack something like this?"

"You start by understanding the mind that created it," Elise replied, her eyes scanning the page. "Look here," she pointed to a segment of the text. "This symbol repeats. In alchemical texts, it often represents transformation or transmutation. That could be a theme or a clue to his motivations."

Leo leaned in closer, trying to follow her thought process. "So, you think Greaves or his killer was trying to transform something, or someone?"

"Maybe. Or it's a metaphorical use, symbolizing change or enlightenment. It's hard to say without more context." Elise sighed, frustration edging into her voice.

Just then, a junior detective, Sarah, entered the lab with a laptop under her arm. "Dr. Bennett, Detective Marquez, you might want to see this. I found something on an online forum about esoteric practices that mentions a user named 'Puppeteer' talking about transformation rituals."

Elise's interest peaked immediately. "Can you bring it up on the screen? Let's see the exact wording."

Sarah nodded, opening the laptop and navigating to the webpage. The forum was filled with discussions on arcane topics, but one thread stood out. It was a detailed post by 'Puppeteer', discussing the symbolic importance of using rituals to achieve a higher state of consciousness.

Leo read over her shoulder. "Does any of this line up with what we found at the crime scene?"

"It might," Elise mused. "These posts discuss using symbols as part of the ritualistic process, which is exactly what we saw on Greaves' body. Whoever this is, they know a lot about the subject, enough to teach it or... orchestrate it."

"Can we trace the post?" Leo asked, turning to Sarah.

"We're trying, but the user is using heavy encryption. We might need more time to break through it," Sarah explained.

"Keep at it," Leo directed before turning back to Elise. "So, what's our next step here?"

"We analyze everything Greaves wrote about these symbols, compare it with this forum material, and see if we can't draw a more direct line between his work and what happened to him," Elise proposed, already moving to collect some of Greaves' papers from another table.

Leo nodded, his mind racing with the implications of their findings. "And I'll start putting together a profile based on this 'Puppeteer' character.

Maybe if we understand him, we can figure out his connection to Greaves."

Elise paused, her hand resting on a stack of papers. "Leo, what if Greaves was part of this? What if he was more involved than just being a victim?"

Leo considered this, his eyes narrowing slightly. "Then we find out how deep he was in, and whether he was trying to get out... or go deeper. Either way, we find this Puppeteer."

Their determination filled the space, a silent agreement that they were on the edge of a deeper darkness than they had anticipated. The morning's light seemed less bright now, overshadowed by the weight of hidden secrets they were only just beginning to uncover.

In the secluded confines of the lab, surrounded by the persistent hum of machinery and the subtle scent of antiseptic, Elise Bennett sat deeply engrossed in a sea of ancient texts and cryptic notes scattered around her. Her eyes, underlined with fatigue, moved methodically between the documents and a digital copy of the symbol-laden manuscript found in Dr. Greaves' possession. She was drawing connections with colored markers, lines weaving across the pages like a spider's web, each one punctuated with annotations in her neat, precise handwriting.

Leo Marquez watched her from across the room, his arms folded as he leaned against a sterile counter. The intensity of her focus was palpable, almost a tangible force in the room. After a long moment, he broke the silence. "You're onto something, aren't you?"

Elise looked up, her gaze momentarily distant as she adjusted to the shift from her thoughts to the present. "I think so," she began, her voice steady despite the underlying excitement. "These symbols, they're not just random or purely ritualistic. They represent a sophisticated understanding of psychological concepts, but twisted, repurposed for something... darker."

Leo pushed off from the counter, stepping closer to examine the web of theories Elise had laid out. "Darker how?"

"Look here," Elise said, pointing to a series of symbols that she had linked to specific psychological theories. "These symbols correlate with stages of human consciousness, according to Jungian psychology—conscious, unconscious, and collective unconscious. But in this context, they seem to be used as a map, a way to manipulate or navigate someone's psyche."

Leo's brow furrowed as he considered the implications. "You're saying the killer is using these as part of the murder method? Like a psychological tool?"

"Exactly," Elise confirmed. "It's as if the ritual and the symbols were meant to enact a psychological transformation or... perhaps a domination. It's speculative still, but I think Greaves might have been experimenting with these ideas, possibly under the influence of this 'Puppeteer.'"

The gravity of her suggestion hung between them, a chilling prospect that added a new layer of complexity to the case. Leo paced a short line before stopping and facing Elise again. "So, this wasn't just a murder; it was an experiment?"

"Possibly," Elise conceded, her tone cautious. "An experiment or a demonstration. We need more information about Greaves' recent activities and communications. Whoever did this, they might have been trying to prove a point to him, or through him."

The discussion paused as Elise turned back to her notes, her mind racing through psychological theories and criminal profiles, trying to stitch them together into a coherent theory. Leo watched her work, his mind equally active with the procedural steps they would need to take next.

"This changes our approach," Leo finally said, breaking the contemplative silence. "We're not just looking for a killer; we're looking for someone who thinks they're a master manipulator, someone who's using psychology as a weapon."

Elise nodded without looking up, her hands busy marking another connection on her chart. "And the first step in any manipulation is understanding your subject. We need to understand both Greaves and this Puppeteer if we're going to figure out how deep this goes."

The room settled into a working silence once more, filled only with the soft scratching of Elise's pen and the distant, muffled sounds of the police station beyond the lab. Each theory Elise developed and each line she drew took them deeper into the psyche of a killer hiding behind a curtain of ancient symbols and psychological experiments, pushing the boundaries of what they knew about motive and murder. As Elise worked, the shadows grew longer in the fading light, mirroring the darkening path their investigation was taking.

In the forensic lab, the air was thick with the tension of brewing theories and the quiet buzz of computers. Elise and Leo stood over the sprawling map of Veridian City, now dotted with significant locations derived from Dr. Greaves' notes and their ongoing investigation.

Leo pointed to a cluster of marks on the eastern side of the city. "These locations are centered around historical sites. It fits the profile you're suggesting—someone deeply entrenched in the past, using it somehow."

Elise nodded, her eyes tracing the lines connecting the dots. "Yes, and it's not just about location. The timing of these meetings or whatever they were, coincides with the lunar phases. It's classic in ritualistic practices, adding another layer of complexity to this."

"That sounds like we're dealing with more than one person," Leo said, his voice laced with frustration. "This is organized, planned to meticulous detail. It's not just the work of a lone madman."

"Exactly, which brings us back to the idea of a group," Elise responded, her tone somber. "Greaves could have been part of it, willingly or not. This 'Puppeteer' figure could be the leader or just another pawn."

Leo crossed his arms, considering. "If Greaves was involved, he might have been trying to get out. That could have been his undoing."

Elise paused, her expression contemplative. "Or he was trying to take control. We can't assume he was a victim until we understand the dynamics of this group."

Their discussion was interrupted by the sound of an incoming email notification from Elise's laptop. She quickly checked the message, a hint of anticipation in her eyes. "It's from the university. They've found a collection of private journals that Greaves kept. They're sending them over."

"That could be the breakthrough we need," Leo said, a spark of hope lighting his features.

Elise smiled slightly, her mind already racing with the possibilities. "Let's hope so."

As they waited for the journals to arrive, the conversation shifted to the practical aspects of their next moves. "We should consider witness protection for anyone close to Greaves who might be at risk," Leo suggested, his tone serious. "If there's a group involved, they won't appreciate us digging around."

Elise agreed, her thoughts on the safety of their potential witnesses. "And we need to be careful too. If this Puppeteer is as dangerous as we think, we're likely already on his radar."

The tension in the room grew as they considered the implications. The arrival of a junior officer with the journals broke the palpable anxiety momentarily. Elise and Leo eagerly opened the first volume, hoping for insights into Greaves' private thoughts and possibly more about the mysterious group.

As they flipped through the pages, Elise's sharp eyes caught a series of entries that shed new light on the situation. "Here," she pointed out, her voice a mix of excitement and concern. "Greaves mentions disagreements within the group. He talks about 'escalating demands' and 'losing sight of the original purpose.'"

Leo leaned over to read the passage. "Sounds like there was internal conflict. That could have led to his murder."

"It's more than that," Elise elaborated, her analytical mind piecing together the narrative. "He mentions feeling threatened, but also determined to redirect the course. It's like he knew he was in danger but believed he could control the outcome."

"The arrogance of thinking he could manipulate a manipulator," Leo mused, a grim note in his voice.

Elise closed the journal, her mind set. "We need to find out who else was in this group. Greaves' arrogance might have led to his death, but it also means he wasn't acting alone. There are others out there."

The room settled into a heavy silence as they absorbed the gravity of their discovery. Each piece of the puzzle added depth to their understanding of the case, but also broadened the shadows in which their adversaries hid. The path forward was clearer now, yet fraught with dangers, as they delved deeper into the cryptic and deadly world of ancient rituals and modern murders.

Elise and Leo were deep in discussion, surrounded by the evidence and artifacts that cluttered the confines of their makeshift command center at the precinct. The journals of Dr. Greaves had opened new avenues of investigation, but it was the link between the cryptic messages and the locations marked on the city map that now held their attention.

Leo, looking over a printout of the forum posts they had found, turned to Elise. "These posts... they're too detailed, too precise to be coincidental. This Puppeteer knew Greaves, or at least his work, very intimately."

Elise, who was cross-referencing the journal entries with dates and symbols from the notes, nodded in agreement. "And look at this entry. Greaves mentions a confrontation at what he calls 'the final gathering'—a term that's come up in several of these journal entries. He seems to have been planning to expose something significant."

"Do we have a date or location for this gathering?" Leo asked, his interest piqued.

"That's just it," Elise replied, her eyes scanning the page. "He was vague about the details, probably for safety. But he does mention 'the old mill on the outskirts' in the context of previous gatherings. Maybe that's our place."

Leo grabbed his phone and started scrolling through his contacts. "I'm going to see if I can push for a warrant to check out this mill. If we're right, it could be a significant piece of the puzzle."

As Leo made calls, Elise's attention was drawn back to her laptop screen by another email notification. Opening it, she found an attachment from the university's IT department—security footage from the campus on the days leading up to Greaves' murder.

"Leo, come over here. You need to see this," Elise called out.

Leo walked over as Elise played the video. It showed Greaves entering a building, followed a few minutes later by a figure in a dark hoodie—the same kind of figure seen in the security footage from near Greaves' office the night he died.

"That has to be our guy," Leo said, pointing at the screen. "Can we enhance the video, get a better look at this person?"

"I'll send it over to tech support, see what they can do," Elise replied, forwarding the video with a few clicks.

As they waited, Elise turned her chair to face Leo. "If this is the Puppeteer, or even an associate, they were stalking Greaves before the murder. They were probably making sure he was going to be alone that night."

Leo, who had resumed his phone conversation, nodded to Elise as he spoke into the receiver. "Yeah, we have possible video evidence linking a suspect to the victim both at the university and the crime scene. We need that warrant expedited."

Hanging up, he gave Elise a grim smile. "Warrant's on its way. We might just catch this Puppeteer sooner than we thought."

Just then, Elise's phone beeped with another alert. She checked it, her expression turning serious. "It's from tech support. They've managed to pull a partial license plate from the car the suspect drove off in after following Greaves."

"That's great! With the car model and this partial plate, we can start tracking down the owner," Leo said, already dialing another number to relay this new information.

The pace in the office picked up as the potential breakthroughs infused the team with a new energy. Leads were followed up with renewed vigor, the collective effort driving them closer to unraveling the mystery.

Leo stepped back, watching the team work. "If we find this car, and it leads us to our Puppeteer, what's your gut say about what we'll find?"

Elise paused, considering the weight of the case. "I think we're about to uncover something big, Leo. This isn't just about one murder; it's about something much darker and deeper."

The room buzzed with activity as they prepared for what might come next, the air charged with anticipation and the gravity of their impending discoveries. Each step forward was now crucial, the threads of the case slowly weaving together to form a clearer picture of the intricate and deadly tapestry in which they found themselves entangled.

Chapter 3
Dr. Bennett's Insight

The morning was unusually brisk as Elise Bennett and Leo Marquez arrived at the old mill, a structure cloaked in the history and shadows of Veridian City's outskirts. The building loomed like a relic of the industrial past, its dilapidated exterior masked by overgrowth that whispered of long neglect. The early light cast stark contrasts across its facade, deepening the sense of foreboding that hung in the air.

As they approached, Elise noted the architecture—stoic, enduring, and fraught with significance. It was the kind of place that could easily become the setting for clandestine meetings or obscure rituals. The historical resonance of the site was palpable, the stones themselves seeming to hold secrets.

Inside, the vast space was cluttered with the remnants of its industrial past. Shafts of light pierced through broken panes, illuminating the dust motes that danced in the still air. Leo led the way with a flashlight, its beam slicing through the darkness, revealing old machinery and piles of decaying wood.

As they delved deeper into the mill, Elise's attention was caught by a series of markings on the inner wall of the main chamber. Unlike the graffiti that sporadically marred the outer areas, these marks were deliberate and ordered. Symbols, similar in style to those found on Greaves' body, were etched into the brickwork, some faded by time, others startlingly clear.

"These look like the symbols in Greaves' notes," Elise murmured, her fingers hovering close but not touching. "See how each one is distinct yet repetitive, forming a pattern? This wasn't the work of vandals; it's too systematic, too purposeful."

Leo examined the markings closely, his expression one of focused contemplation. "Do you think this was a meeting place for that group you mentioned? The one Greaves might have been involved with?"

"It's possible," Elise replied, stepping back to view the arrangements from a different angle. "These symbols could have been used in their rituals or as a means of communicating secret knowledge among members."

They continued their exploration, moving through areas that felt untouched by time. In a smaller, secluded room off the main chamber, they discovered a collection of old, leather-bound books. Each volume was dense with handwritten notes and drawings that echoed the symbols on the wall and in Greaves' book.

Elise carefully opened one of the books, her gloves protecting the brittle pages from further wear. The writings inside were complex, discussing psychological and philosophical concepts that tied back to the notions of transformation and transcendence—themes that were becoming a central thread of their investigation.

"The historical significance of this place isn't just architectural," Elise noted as she carefully turned another page. "It's imbued with the intellectual and esoteric pursuits of those who congregated here. This wasn't merely a mill; it was a meeting ground for minds enthralled by the arcane."

The realization brought them both a sense of clarity and unease. The connection between the physical and the metaphysical, the past and the present, was becoming increasingly tangible. The symbols, the notes, the secluded location—all pointed to a concerted effort to cloak their activities in secrecy.

As they prepared to leave, Elise took one last look around, the weight of their discovery pressing upon her. The mill, with its hidden rooms and secret knowledge, was a testament to the depth of the mystery they were unraveling. It was a place where history whispered through the walls, and where each shadow seemed to hold a fragment of the truth they sought.

Outside, the light had shifted, casting longer shadows that seemed to reach out towards them as they made their way back to the car. The morning's discoveries had deepened the case, weaving the historical into the criminal, and setting the stage for the revelations yet to come.

After leaving the old mill, Elise and Leo returned to the precinct. The car ride had been quiet, each lost in thought over the discoveries of the morning. Upon arriving, Elise retreated to her temporary office, a small room lined with bookshelves filled with psychological texts and criminological reports. Sitting at her desk, she picked up a worn book, a collection of essays on psychoanalytic theory that she had used during her university days. The sight and feel of the book transported her back to those formative years.

Elise had been an eager student, her fascination with the human psyche driving her to delve into the most complex theories. She remembered long nights spent in the university library, the silence broken only by the occasional rustle of pages turning or the distant sound of footsteps echoing through the halls.

One evening, as rain battered the library windows, she had found herself deep in the stacks, a section seldom visited by others, where the oldest psychology books were kept. She had pulled a particularly old book from the shelf, its leather cover cracked and pages yellowed with age. As she flipped through, she stumbled upon a chapter discussing symbolic interactionism and the use of symbols in altering self-concept and reality. The theories had fascinated her then, and now they seemed eerily relevant.

Her reverie was interrupted by a knock at the door. It was Leo, holding a couple of coffee cups. He handed her one as he sat down across from her.

"Lost in thought?" he asked, taking a sip of his coffee.

Elise smiled faintly, placing the old book on the desk. "Just remembering something from my university days. I spent hours in the library, just like Greaves, lost in these theories that most found too esoteric."

Leo looked at the book. "Anything in there that can help us now?"

"Possibly," Elise said, opening the book to a marked page. "I was drawn to the use of symbols in psychological practices. It's fascinating how symbols can influence perception and even reality for some. Greaves might have been experimenting with these concepts, pushing them further than just theory."

Leo leaned forward, intrigued. "So, he could have been trying to use these symbols to manipulate reality? Like, creating a new reality for his group or himself?"

"Exactly," Elise nodded. "And if the Puppeteer took over, it could have been to steer that reality in a direction Greaves wasn't willing to go."

"That's a strong motive for murder," Leo mused, his brow furrowing. "To control the narrative, the reality they were creating."

Elise sipped her coffee, her mind working through the implications. "It's about power. Whoever controls the symbols, controls the reality. Greaves lost control, or maybe he saw the dangers and wanted to stop."

"Which means," Leo added, "that whoever is behind this, they're not just killing. They're creating, manipulating on a level we've barely touched."

The gravity of the situation settled between them, the pieces of the puzzle not just forming a picture of a crime, but of a profound manipulation of minds and realities.

Elise closed the book and looked at Leo. "We need to go deeper into Greaves' recent activities, find out who he was meeting, what they were discussing. And we need to find this Puppeteer before they can orchestrate anything else."

Leo stood, his resolve firm. "Let's dig into Greaves' communications, his meetings. Anyone he was close to at the university could be a key to unlocking this."

Elise nodded, her determination matching Leo's. "I'll start with his academic circle. There's a conference next week where he was supposed to speak. It might be a good place to look for connections."

As Leo left to follow up on their leads, Elise turned her attention back to the book, the theories within now more than just academic interest. They were clues to understanding a murderer who operated not just outside the law, but outside the very boundaries of reality as most knew it.

Back in her office filled with the growing mountain of case files and research material, Dr. Elise Bennett found herself poring over a whiteboard filled with names, dates, and locations, all tied to Dr. Greaves and the mysterious Puppeteer. Each piece of information was a dot on the map of this complex investigation. As she stepped back to assess the web of connections, Detective Leo Marquez walked in, his hands filled with papers.

"Found something interesting in Greaves' phone records," Leo announced, laying the documents on Elise's already cluttered desk. "He made several calls to a now-defunct bookstore known for its collection of esoteric and occult texts. Might be worth looking into who else was shopping for similar materials."

Elise perked up at this. "That could give us another angle on who might be in his circle of influence. Did you get names?"

"A few," Leo said, flipping through his notes. "I'm waiting on a full list, but the owner was cooperative. Seems Greaves wasn't the only psychologist making regular visits."

"That ties back to the theory that this group might be larger than just a few isolated academics," Elise noted, adding this new information to the board. "We need to track down every one of these individuals. They might not all be directly involved, but even tangential connections could shed light on Greaves' activities."

Leo nodded in agreement. "I'll see if we can prioritize those names, maybe pull some favors with the data analysis team."

As they discussed their next steps, Sarah, the junior detective working under Leo, knocked and entered with her laptop open. "You might want to see this," she said, her expression serious. "I managed to pull some encrypted emails from Greaves' account that were flagged as suspicious. Took some doing to crack the encryption, but there's a thread discussing a meeting about 'reaching the next level of understanding.'"

Elise leaned in, intrigued. "Can you trace the other participants in the thread?"

"Working on it," Sarah replied. "But the language is coded. They're using a lot of metaphors—something about 'weaving the fabric of reality' and 'mastering the threads.'"

"That's consistent with the symbolism we've been seeing," Elise mused, tapping the whiteboard where she had drawn connections between various symbols found in Greaves' notes and the crime scene. "This isn't just academic theory; they're practically applying these concepts."

Leo, looking over the emails, frowned. "This is getting deeper than just a study group gone wrong. We're looking at a cult-like behavior pattern here, with Greaves possibly trying to back out or take over."

"The dynamics of power within such groups can be volatile," Elise added. "If Greaves was seen as a threat to this Puppeteer, it would explain the drastic response."

"Murder as a ritualistic silencing," Leo concluded grimly.

Elise nodded slowly, her eyes scanning the board. "And if we're right about the bookstore connection, we might find they were sourcing materials to enhance their rituals or meetings—maybe even recruiting."

The room fell silent for a moment as the weight of their discoveries settled. The connections were becoming clearer, each piece of evidence adding to the grim tapestry of manipulation and control woven by the group Greaves had entangled himself with.

"Let's organize a visit to that bookstore," Elise suggested, turning back to her computer to schedule the trip. "Seeing the place firsthand might give us more insight into what Greaves was after, or who else was involved."

Leo agreed, pulling out his phone to arrange the details. "I'll get a team ready. If this place was a hub for them, it might be risky."

As Leo and Sarah prepared for the next phase of their investigation, Elise remained at her desk, her thoughts deep in the complexity of the case. Each lead, each connection added more depth to the narrative they were uncovering, painting a picture of a dark and intricate plot that had claimed at least one life and threatened to engulf more.

In the subdued light of her office, Elise Bennett shuffled through the latest batch of documents—a mix of ancient book receipts, forum communications, and notes from their last field visit to the mysterious bookstore. The walls of the room were plastered with evidence boards and photos connected by strings that formed a complex web of relationships and events.

As Leo Marquez entered, he noticed the intensity in Elise's gaze, fixated on a particular set of symbols she had drawn on a large pad of paper. "Find something new?" he asked, setting down two cups of coffee on the desk.

"Yes, something potentially big," Elise replied, accepting the coffee with a nod of gratitude. She pointed to the symbols. "These aren't just random markings. They're part of a larger system, a kind of linguistic framework used to convey complex philosophical ideas. I think Greaves and his group were trying to use these as a sort of psychological programming language."

Leo leaned in to get a better look. "Programming? Like in computers?"

"In a way, yes," Elise explained, her finger tracing the lines and circles of the symbols. "But more in terms of programming reality—altering perceptions, embedding certain thought patterns, or beliefs into the subconscious. It's an extension of Greaves' work on the influence of symbols on the psyche but taken to a much more active, deliberate level."

Leo looked puzzled but intrigued. "So, you're suggesting they were trying to use these symbols to control people? To make them see the world differently, or even control their actions?"

"Exactly," Elise confirmed, her voice filled with a mixture of excitement and trepidation. "It's speculative, but I believe this could be what Greaves was ultimately killed for—either he was trying to push this theory too far, or he wanted to stop it and was silenced."

"That's a leap, but with everything we've seen, it fits," Leo conceded. He sipped his coffee, thinking it over. "If they were experimenting with this kind of mental manipulation, it could have serious implications. We might be dealing with a group that's capable of influencing or controlling people at a level we haven't seen before."

Elise nodded, her mind racing with the potential scope of their discovery. "And if this Puppeteer is at the center of it, he could be more dangerous than we thought. Not just a murderer, but someone who can manipulate minds, make people do things..."

"We need solid proof," Leo said, his expression hardening with the resolve. "Something more concrete than theoretical applications of psychological research. Have you got anything that ties these theories directly to Greaves' activities?"

"Not yet," Elise admitted, tapping her pen against the notebook. "But I have a meeting set up with one of his former colleagues tomorrow. Someone who was working closely with him on a project that seems to have involved these practices."

"That could be our break," Leo said, already reaching for his phone to ensure backup for the meeting. "I'll make sure we're prepared for anything."

Elise smiled, appreciative of Leo's protective instincts. "Thanks, Leo. I think we're really onto something here."

As Leo left the office, Elise turned back to her boards, her eyes scanning the interconnected web of evidence. Each symbol, each line of inquiry, brought them closer to understanding the true nature of the Puppeteer's influence. The implications of such psychological control were daunting, but Elise was determined to uncover the truth, no matter how deep she had to dig or how dark the answers might be.

The city outside was settling into the evening, lights flickering on as the shadows lengthened. Inside, the glow from Elise's desk lamp cast a warm island of light in a sea of gathering darkness, a beacon as she navigated the murky waters of their investigation.

Chapter 4
First Lead

In the dimly lit corridors beneath Veridian's grand public library, a hidden world of archives sprawled—an ancient repository of forgotten books and manuscripts. The air was thick with the must of old paper and the weight of hidden histories. Detective Leo Marquez and Dr. Elise Bennett followed the faint hum of an air conditioner to a heavy wooden door, beyond which awaited The Archivist.

The room they entered was lined with towering shelves, each filled to the brim with aging documents and leather-bound volumes. At the center, surrounded by piles of books and scrolls, sat an elderly man with spectacles perched precariously on the bridge of his nose. He looked up as they approached, his eyes sharp and assessing.

"Dr. Bennett, Detective Marquez, I presume?" the man spoke first, his voice a gravelly echo in the quiet of the archives.

"Yes, I'm Dr. Bennett and this is Detective Marquez. You must be Mr. Hawthorne, the archivist?" Elise extended her hand, which the old man shook with a surprisingly firm grip.

"Indeed, I am," he confirmed, gesturing for them to sit. "I understand you're here about the... unusual aspects of Dr. Greaves' research?"

"That's correct, Mr. Hawthorne," Leo interjected. "We believe that some of the materials Dr. Greaves might have used could be found in this archive. His work seems to have intersected with some very old psychological theories and practices."

Hawthorne nodded thoughtfully, steepling his fingers. "Yes, Greaves was here often. He had a particular interest in our collection of early psychological texts, especially those concerning the symbolic interaction between the conscious and unconscious mind. Quite fascinating, really, if a bit esoteric for my taste."

"Did he access materials that were not part of the general collection? Something more... restricted?" Elise asked, leaning forward slightly.

The Archivist's eyes twinkled behind his glasses as he leaned back. "Indeed, he had permissions for our special collections. Rare books that require careful handling and are not listed in the general catalog. Are you interested in viewing these materials?"

"We are," Leo confirmed. "And we're particularly interested in any books or documents that deal with symbols or rituals."

"Ah, the rituals," Hawthorne murmured, pushing himself up from his chair. He moved to a large cabinet in the corner of the room and retrieved a small, dusty key from his pocket. "Follow me."

They trailed behind him to a secluded section of the archive, where he unlocked a large metal gate that screeched softly as it swung open. Inside, the air was cooler, the silence more profound.

"This section houses some of the oldest and most delicate items in our collection," Hawthorne explained as he led them to a small table where several books lay covered with dark cloth.

He carefully unveiled one, a thick tome bound in dark leather with intricate engravings. "This book, for example, dates back to the 17th century. It's a detailed study of psychological rituals used by early practitioners who believed that certain symbols and rites could influence the human psyche in profound ways."

Elise examined the book carefully, her eyes scanning the open page filled with detailed diagrams and notes in the margins. "This is exactly what we're looking for. These symbols here," she pointed, "they match some of the symbols we found in Greaves' notes."

Hawthorne looked over her shoulder, nodding. "Yes, Greaves was quite taken with that volume. He consulted it frequently over the last few months."

"Do you know if he met with anyone else here? Perhaps someone with similar interests?" Leo asked, watching the Archivist closely.

"Not to my knowledge," Hawthorne replied after a pause. "But then, I merely oversee the collections. I don't monitor the scholars' comings and goings too closely."

"Thank you, Mr. Hawthorne. Your help has been invaluable," Elise said, her mind already racing with the implications of their findings.

As they prepared to leave, Hawthorne handed Elise a small card. "If you need further assistance, don't hesitate to contact me. There's much more here that might be of interest to your investigation."

Stepping out of the archive, the light of the day seemed harsh after the gloom of the underground. Elise and Leo exchanged a look of shared resolve. The old books had opened new avenues in their quest to understand Greaves' murder—avenues that seemed to stretch deep into the shadows of the human mind.

After their enlightening conversation with Mr. Hawthorne, Elise Bennett and Leo Marquez were left alone in the restricted section of the archives, the air around them heavy with the scent of aging paper and leather. The Archivist had returned to his duties, leaving them to explore the trove of rare and esoteric texts that might hold the key to understanding the more arcane aspects of Dr. Greaves' research and possible murder.

Leo watched as Elise carefully turned the pages of a particularly old tome, her expression one of concentrated curiosity. "Anything that looks promising?" he asked, peering over her shoulder at the complex diagrams and faded text.

Elise paused on a page, her finger tracing a series of intricate symbols. "This could be significant," she said, pointing at a detailed illustration that mirrored one of the symbols found at the crime scene. "This symbol is associated with transformation and control within the psyche, according to the text. It's exactly the sort of thing Greaves was obsessed with."

"Can you make out what it says about how it was used?" Leo asked, his voice low in the quiet of the archive.

"It seems to be part of a larger ritual," Elise replied, squinting at the old script. "It says here that the symbol was used to 'bind the shadow self, allowing the true essence to emerge unimpeded.' It's metaphorical but could be interpreted as a way to manipulate or even erase parts of a person's personality."

Leo raised his eyebrows. "That sounds like it could be dangerous if misused. Do you think Greaves was trying something like that?"

"Possibly," Elise considered, turning another page. "It's hard to say without knowing more about the specifics of his experiments, but this could definitely be part of it."

As Elise continued to examine the book, Leo moved to another section of shelves, pulling down another volume that looked promising. "This one's on ancient rites of knowledge and power," he announced, flipping through the dust-covered pages. "There's a whole chapter on using symbols in group settings to enhance the collective consciousness."

"That aligns with the idea of Greaves being involved in a group that was experimenting with these concepts," Elise noted, joining Leo to look at the book he had found. "Does it mention anything about the risks or consequences of these rites?"

Leo scanned the text, his finger following the lines. "Yes, here it says that 'the unprepared mind can be overwhelmed or shattered by the forces invoked.' That sounds like it could lead to serious psychological damage."

"Which might explain why someone wanted Greaves dead," Elise mused. "If he was trying to back out or shut down the experiments because of the dangers involved."

The duo exchanged a sobering glance, the implications of their findings casting a shadow over their investigation. They were delving into dangerous territory, where the quest for knowledge could easily slip into the realm of psychological warfare.

"I'll take pictures of these pages," Elise said, pulling out her phone. "We'll need to go over them in more detail back at the precinct and see how they connect with the other evidence."

Leo nodded in agreement, helping her photograph the key pages of both books. "I think we should also check if there are any living relatives or close associates of Greaves who might know more about his activities," he suggested. "Someone must have known what he was getting into."

"Good idea," Elise agreed as they finished their work. "Let's head back. We have a lot to go through, and I have a feeling we're just scratching the surface."

As they left the cool darkness of the archive, stepping back into the light of day, the weight of history and knowledge they carried with them felt tangible, a crucial piece of the puzzle in their hands, yet so much remained hidden, waiting to be uncovered.

After documenting their findings, Elise and Leo made their way back to the main office of the archives, where Mr. Hawthorne awaited them, his demeanor displaying a mix of curiosity and concern.

"Did you find what you were looking for?" the Archivist asked as they approached his desk, his eyes keenly observing the expressions on their faces.

"Yes, and possibly more," Elise replied, placing her notes carefully on the desk. "The texts were incredibly informative. They align closely with some of the psychological theories Dr. Greaves was working on."

"I'm glad to hear they were useful," Mr. Hawthorne responded, his fingers tented before him. "However, I must caution you both. The knowledge contained in those books is powerful and, in the wrong hands, potentially dangerous."

Leo, who had been quietly listening, spoke up. "We're beginning to see that. It seems Dr. Greaves might have been involved in something that went beyond academic research."

Mr. Hawthorne nodded gravely. "I suspected as much. He was a frequent visitor here and often requested materials that were... unorthodox, even by scholarly standards. His interest seemed to deepen over time, almost to the point of obsession."

"Did he ever speak to you about his work?" Elise asked, her notebook ready to capture any additional insights.

"Not in detail," Hawthorne admitted. "But he did once mention that his research was reaching a point where he felt the lines between theoretical and practical application were blurring. He seemed both exhilarated and troubled by the implications of his findings."

"That matches our understanding," Elise noted, scribbling down Hawthorne's words. "Did he ever express any concerns for his safety or mention any individuals who might have opposed his work?"

"Not specifically," the Archivist replied. "But there was an undertone of urgency and caution in his later visits. He once asked about the security of our archive—whether our logs of who accessed certain materials were secure."

Leo leaned forward slightly, intrigued by this new information. "Security? Was he worried someone might find out what he was accessing?"

"Possibly," Hawthorne said, leaning back in his chair. "He didn't elaborate, but it was clear that discretion had become a priority for him."

Elise exchanged a quick glance with Leo before turning back to Hawthorne. "If there's anything else you can remember—any detail, no matter how small—it could be crucial to our investigation."

Mr. Hawthorne paused, considering their request seriously. "I will certainly let you know if I recall anything else. In the meantime, I must urge you both to tread carefully. The subjects of these texts are not just historical footnotes. They can have real, profound effects on individuals unprepared for their depths."

"We understand," Leo assured him. "And we appreciate your help and your caution."

As they prepared to leave, Mr. Hawthorne stood and extended his hand. "Be mindful of the shadows you stir. Some are darker than the ink on these pages."

Elise nodded, feeling the weight of his words. "We will. Thank you, Mr. Hawthorne."

With that, they left the archives, the warning echoing in their minds. The drive back to the precinct was quiet, each absorbed in their thoughts about the deepening complexities of the case. The information they had gathered was a significant lead, yet the Archivist's cautionary words lingered, a somber reminder of the delicate balance between seeking knowledge and awakening dangers.

Back at the precinct, Elise and Leo settled into the task force room, strewn with maps and documents. Their minds were still reverberating with Mr. Hawthorne's cryptic admonitions as they prepared to sift through the day's findings.

Elise, poring over her notes, paused, her gaze fixing on a particular entry. "Leo, listen to this," she said, her tone indicating a breakthrough. "According to one of these notes from the archives, there's a reference to an event scheduled to occur at 'the old Wilson estate'—it's described here as a culmination of their efforts. This has to be connected to the group Greaves was involved with."

Leo perked up, his investigative instincts kicking in. "The Wilson estate? Isn't that the place that was seized by the city last year due to unpaid taxes? It's been empty since then."

"Exactly," Elise replied, her eyes alight with the potential of this lead. "It's isolated, historic, and currently empty—perfect for something secretive. This could very well be where the group is planning their next... whatever it is they're planning."

Leo grabbed his phone, quickly dialing their field team. "I'm sending a team to scout the Wilson estate. We need eyes on the place ASAP. If this is their next meeting spot, we might catch them in the act."

Elise nodded in agreement, her mind racing ahead. "I'll pull up everything we have on the estate—any recent activities, permits filed, anything that might give us more insight."

As they waited for updates, Leo looked over to Elise. "Do you think this is where they're planning another ritual?"

"It's highly possible," Elise considered, tapping her fingers against her notebook. "The timing fits, and if they're as ambitious as Hawthorne suggested, they'll want a dramatic setting for whatever they're planning."

Not long after, a call came in from the field team. Leo answered on speakerphone so Elise could listen. "We're at the Wilson estate now," reported the team leader, Detective Harris. "Place is quiet from the outside, but we're going to do a full perimeter check."

"Look for any signs of recent activity," Leo directed. "Tracks, lights, anything out of place. And be discreet—we don't know what we're dealing with yet."

"Understood," Harris replied. After a pause, his voice came back, tenser this time. "Wait, we've got something. There's a light on in one of the back rooms. Looks like it's been covered up, but it's definitely a light."

Elise exchanged a sharp look with Leo. "Harris, do not engage. Keep your distance and maintain surveillance. We don't know how many people are inside or what their capabilities are."

"Roger that," Harris confirmed, his voice low and cautious. "We'll keep a watch and report any changes."

Leo ended the call, his expression grim but determined. "This is it, Elise. Whatever is happening, it's happening now. We need to move fast."

Elise closed her notebook, her decision made. "I'll coordinate with the SWAT team and get an operations plan in place. We need to be ready to move as soon as we have enough information."

As they organized the rapid response, the precinct buzzed with the tension and urgency of imminent action. The clue at the Wilson estate had ignited a fuse, and now they were racing against time to prevent whatever the group had planned. Their meticulous investigation had led them here, and as the evening shadows grew longer, so did the shadows of the case, deepening into a darkness they were determined to illuminate.

Chapter 5
Another Victim

The drive to the old Wilson estate was tense and silent, marked only by the occasional crackle of the radio as updates poured in. Elise Bennett and Leo Marquez were both focused, their expressions taut with anticipation. The estate, notorious for its sprawling grounds and dilapidated structure, loomed in their future—a potential site of another sinister event.

As they approached the perimeter, Leo spoke into his radio, coordinating with the teams already in place. "Harris, status update?"

Detective Harris' voice came through, clear despite the static. "We've established a perimeter. No movement in or out since the last update. Light's still on in the same room."

"Any signs of the ritual being set up?" Elise asked, her voice sharp with urgency.

"Not from what we can see," Harris replied. "We need to get inside for a better look, but we're holding position until you arrive."

As they turned off the main road onto the narrow path that led to the estate, the headlights of their vehicle sliced through the darkness, revealing the eerie silhouette of the Wilson estate against the night sky. The building looked desolate, its windows dark except for the one faint light they had been told about.

Leo parked the car a safe distance away, and they quickly joined Harris and the rest of the team. "Show me where the light is," Leo commanded, pulling out a map of the building layout that they had studied earlier.

Harris pointed to a section on the map, then to the corresponding part of the house visible from their position. "It's there, second floor, west wing.

That part of the house was supposed to be sealed off according to the records."

Elise peered through her binoculars, trying to get a better view. "There's something off about that light. It's too deliberate, like it's meant to be seen."

"Could be a trap," Leo muttered, his hand instinctively resting on his weapon.

"Or a signal," Elise countered, lowering her binoculars. "They might be communicating with someone outside, or it could be a distraction."

"We can't take any chances," Leo decided. "We move in quietly, Harris, take your team to the back entrance. Elise and I will go in from the side. We need to approach from multiple angles to cover more ground."

Harris nodded, his team readying their gear. "Got it. We'll be on comms."

As they split up, Elise pulled Leo aside. "If this is another ritual site, there might be more than just the group to worry about. These rituals can... affect the mind. We need to be prepared for anything."

Leo nodded, his expression grave. "I know. Watch your back in there."

They approached the side entrance, the old wood of the door groaning under Leo's careful push. Inside, the air was musty, filled with the scent of decay and old secrets. The house was silent except for the distant sound of their team members moving stealthily.

As they made their way to the staircase leading to the second floor, every step creaked ominously under their weight. "This place gives me the creeps," Leo whispered, his flashlight beam dancing across peeling wallpaper and dusty portraits.

"Focus on the mission," Elise whispered back, her own light scanning the shadows for any movement or signs of recent activity.

They reached the second floor, and the light from the room was now visible down the hallway, spilling out from beneath a door left slightly ajar. Leo gestured for Elise to stay back as he approached, pressing his ear against the wood to listen for any sounds.

Silence.

He pushed the door open slowly, gun raised, ready for anything. But the room was empty, except for a single candle burning on a small table, surrounded by strange symbols and an open book.

Elise stepped in beside him, her eyes scanning the setup. "No one's here, but look at this arrangement. It's almost identical to what we found at Greaves' murder scene."

Leo's voice was low and tense. "They were here, and recently. This might have been a rehearsal... or a failed attempt."

As they stood there, the reality of how close they might be to preventing another tragedy—or walking into a trap—settled over them like the dust that coated everything in the decrepit room.

The stillness of the old Wilson estate was deceptive, a quiet that seemed almost loud to Elise and Leo as they processed the scene before them. They were in what once must have been a lavish dining room, now a stage for a sinister tableau. The room, illuminated by the stark light of police flashlights, revealed walls that were faded replicas of their former glory, the wallpaper peeling like aged skin. Amidst this decay, the remains of a new crime scene were grotesquely displayed.

The body was positioned in the center of the room, surrounded by a circle of candles that had burned down to stubs, their wax spilling out onto the tarnished wooden floor like drops of time. Symbols similar to those found in the books from the archives had been drawn around the perimeter in a chalky substance, their meanings obscure yet undeniably ominous.

Elise knelt beside the body, her gloves snapping on with the crisp sound of efficiency. The victim, a middle-aged man, bore an expression of terror, frozen on his face as if he had seen something unimaginable at the moment of his death. There were no visible wounds; it was as if his life had been scared out of him, a fact that would only be confirmed or denied by the autopsy.

"Looks like he was part of the ritual, willingly or not," Elise murmured, examining the arrangement of items around the body. Each object seemed to have been placed with deliberate care, contributing to a ritualistic pattern that suggested both an offering and a binding.

Leo, standing watchful guard, noted the precision in the setup. "This wasn't the work of amateurs. Whoever did this knew exactly what they were doing, and what they wanted to achieve."

The air was thick with the scent of burnt candle wax and a faint, almost imperceptible aroma of herbs or flowers that might have been part of the ritual. As Elise continued her examination, she found a small, leather-bound book clutched in the victim's hand. Carefully prying it free, she opened it to reveal notes and sketches that mirrored those in Greaves' research, suggesting that the victim was not just a participant but perhaps an active member of the group involved in these dark practices.

"This wasn't just murder; it was a message," Elise concluded, her voice low as she shared her insights with Leo.

As they prepared to move the body, a subtle shift in the air drew Leo's attention to the far corner of the room. With a gesture for Elise to stay back, he approached, flashlight leading the way. Behind a heavy, moth-eaten curtain, he discovered a small alcove with a setup that chilled him to the bone—a shrine of sorts, with photographs of several individuals, some crossed out, others still visible. Among them was a photo of Dr. Greaves, marked with a red 'X'.

The implications were immediate and disturbing. "Elise, you need to see this," he called, keeping his voice steady despite the surge of adrenaline.

Elise joined him, her gaze taking in the shrine. "It's a hit list," she stated flatly, the realization darkening her already grim expression. "Greaves was just one of many targets."

They stood together in the dim light, surrounded by the echoes of the past and the very present threat of a mystery that was unraveling thread by ominous thread. The crime scene before them was not just the aftermath of a ritualistic killing; it was a portal into a labyrinth of motives and shadows, each twist and turn leading them deeper into the heart of a conspiracy that threatened to engulf them as much as it had its victims.

As they stepped out of the room, the weight of their discovery pressed heavily upon them, each piece of evidence a somber note in the symphony of horrors they were piecing together. The night outside was silent, but the quiet felt like the calm before a storm, with Elise and Leo standing on the precipice, looking into the darkness that awaited them.

Back at the precinct, Elise Bennett and Leo Marquez poured over the evidence gathered from the old Wilson estate, spreading everything across a large table that was quickly becoming cluttered with notes, photographs, and various documents.

"The symbols drawn around the body," Elise began, pointing to high-resolution photos they had taken of the crime scene, "they're not just random occult symbols. They correspond closely with the ones we saw in the books from the archive. This ties the ritual directly to the research Greaves was doing."

Leo, who was examining the photographs of the shrine, nodded in agreement. "And look at this," he said, passing a photo to Elise. "The shrine with the photos—every crossed-out face corresponds to a known disappearance or unexplained death we've been tracking. Greaves' face being crossed out confirms he was a target, not just involved."

Elise took the photo, her eyes scanning the details. "This is organized and premeditated. It's like they're marking their achievements. Do we have identities on all the other faces?"

"We're still working on a few, but most are academics or people involved in esoteric studies. It seems like this group targets individuals who delve too deeply into certain areas," Leo explained, his voice tense with the implication.

Elise sighed, her mind racing with the implications. "We need to warn anyone who might be at risk. Anyone who's had contact with Greaves or shown interest in similar research."

"I'll coordinate with the other departments, see if we can get protective details on them ASAP," Leo said, reaching for his phone.

As they continued to discuss their strategy, Elise picked up the small, leather-bound book found with the victim. "This journal might help us understand more about the victim's role," she mused, flipping through the pages. "Look, these entries—some of them describe the rituals in detail, others seem to be personal reflections. It's like he was trying to rationalize what they were doing."

Leo leaned over to look. "Any mention of other members or locations?"

"There are references to meetings and planning sessions, but no names, just initials. And here," she pointed at a passage, "he mentions a 'final event' that would 'elevate them to the next level of understanding.' It's scheduled soon, according to the date here."

"That must be what they were preparing for at the Wilson estate," Leo deduced, his expression darkening. "We might have just scratched the surface of what they're planning."

Elise closed the journal, her features set in determination. "We need to figure out where this final event is going to take place. If we can stop it, we might be able to end this for good."

Leo agreed, standing up to stretch his back. "I'll get the tech team to enhance the images from the shrine, see if we can get clearer shots of the other photos, maybe match them to missing persons or known associates."

"And I'll dive deeper into this journal, see if there's anything else we missed that could lead us to their next move," Elise added, already pulling her laptop closer to start transcribing the entries.

As they worked in tandem, the room filled with a palpable urgency. Each clue they uncovered was a step closer to understanding the shadowy group's intentions, but also a reminder of the stakes involved. Outside, the city continued its restless hum, oblivious to the dark currents swirling through its underbelly, currents that Elise and Leo were determined to expose and sever before any more lives could be claimed by the twisted rituals of a hidden cabal.

The atmosphere in the precinct was charged as Elise Bennett and Leo Marquez worked late into the night, the glow from their laptops casting long shadows across the room. Their investigation had unearthed disturbing layers of a conspiracy woven with threads of arcane knowledge and human vulnerability, and the weight of their discoveries pressed heavily on them.

Leo rubbed his eyes, weary from hours of cross-referencing databases and enhancing images from the shrine. "We've identified two more faces from the shrine," he announced, turning his screen to show Elise. "Both are local academics, specialists in mythological symbolism. They were reported missing last week."

Elise, her notes from the victim's journal spread out before her, nodded grimly. "It fits the pattern. The group targets those who are not just curious but deeply involved in esoteric studies. It's like they're gathering experts for their rituals, or worse, silencing those who might oppose them."

"This isn't just a cult," Leo said, his voice low, reflecting the gravity of their situation. "It's a calculated operation, using fear and manipulation to control its members and eliminate threats."

Elise leaned back, processing this. "And according to this journal, the group believes these rituals grant them insights into controlling reality itself. It's delusional, but the danger is very real."

The room fell silent for a moment, the only sound the hum of the computer fans and the distant murmur of the city outside. Leo finally broke the silence. "What's our next move? We've got potential targets who need protection, and this 'final event' looming."

"We tighten security around the identified targets and keep digging for the location of the final event," Elise responded, her determination clear despite the fatigue etching her features. "We also need to get more from the academics in this field. Someone must know something that can lead us directly to the leaders of this group."

Leo nodded, already drafting requests for interviews with the experts they needed to talk to. "I'll get those interviews set up first thing tomorrow. We need all the insight we can get."

"And I'll revisit the symbols and rituals mentioned in this journal," Elise said, tapping the leather-bound book. "There might be a clue we missed, something about how they choose their locations or times for these events."

As they continued their work, the pieces of the puzzle slowly began to form a clearer picture, though the full scope of the conspiracy remained shrouded in mystery. The reality they were confronting was one of darkness twisted around the cores of history and myth, a perversion of scholarly pursuit turned into something malevolent.

Elise paused, her eyes scanning over a particularly troubling entry in the journal. "Leo, listen to this," she said, her voice steady despite the chill the words brought. "The entry describes a ritual that's supposed to 'unbind the world's veil.' It's scheduled for the next full moon, which is in three days."

"That has to be the final event," Leo concluded, his tone urgent. "If they believe it will give them the power they want, there's no telling what they might do to ensure it happens."

"We need to find where it's going to take place," Elise said, her mind already racing with the logistical challenges of stopping a ritual they had yet to locate.

The task ahead was daunting, but as they packed up their materials for the night, there was a sense of resolve between them. They were more than just law enforcement officers chasing a case; they were the thin line standing against a threat woven through the very fabric of their city's hidden histories.

As they left the precinct, the city around them felt different, shadows seeming deeper and the night air carrying the weight of unseen forces. Yet, the resolve in Elise and Leo's steps spoke of their commitment to illuminate the darkness, no matter what truths awaited them in the light.

Chapter 6
Uncovering The Order

The day had barely begun when Elise Bennett and Leo Marquez reconvened in their usual corner of the precinct, surrounded by a growing landscape of papers, photos, and digital screens. At the center of their focus lay a cryptic note, discovered tucked within the pages of the leather-bound journal they had recovered from the latest crime scene.

"This note—it's written in a combination of arcane symbols and Latin," Elise said, her brow furrowed as she magnified the image on her tablet. "It seems to be a directive for the ritual we believe is planned for the next full moon."

Leo, peering over her shoulder, added, "Can you make out what it's instructing?"

"Some of it," Elise replied, tapping on sections of the digital image to enhance the visibility. "It mentions 'the alignment of stars' and 'the confluence of energies.' Typical esoteric stuff, but it's the specifics that are concerning. It talks about a gathering of the chosen, and a sacrifice."

"Sacrifice?" Leo's voice sharpened with concern. "Does it specify what kind of sacrifice?"

"Not explicitly," Elise answered, shaking her head. "But given what we've seen, it's not going to be just symbolic."

"We need to figure out where this is going to happen," Leo said, his hands clenching slightly. "Have you gotten anything back from the linguistics team on the other parts of the note?"

"They're still working on it," Elise responded, her fingers flying over her keyboard to send a follow-up email. "But they confirmed that the language structure suggests a high level of ceremonial importance. This isn't just a fringe group; it's organized and deeply rooted in whatever belief system they've concocted."

As they spoke, Detective Harris walked up, a sheaf of papers in hand. "Got something you'll want to see," he announced, laying the documents on the table. "Traffic cams picked up some of the known associates of our suspects heading towards the northern outskirts of the city. There's an old estate there, mostly abandoned—fits the profile of places they've used before."

Elise glanced at Leo, then back at Harris. "Good work. We need to surveil that estate without being noticed. If it's their next meeting spot, we can't tip them off that we're onto them."

Leo nodded in agreement. "Harris, coordinate with surveillance. I want eyes on that estate around the clock."

"Will do," Harris replied, turning to leave.

Elise returned her attention to the note. "There's more here," she continued, pointing to a particularly dense cluster of symbols. "This passage seems to be a key part of the ritual. It's repeated several times throughout the note. If we can decode this, we might understand more about their objectives."

"Any idea what it's about?" Leo asked, leaning closer to look.

"It's esoteric, but it revolves around the idea of doorways or gateways," Elise deciphered, her eyes scanning the text. "The symbols are associated with thresholds, not just physical but metaphysical. They might believe this ritual will open something, or summon something."

"That's unsettling," Leo muttered, rubbing the back of his neck. "Opening doorways to what, exactly?"

"That's what we need to find out," Elise said. "I'll send this section to the linguistics team as a priority. Whatever they're planning, it sounds like it's not just dangerous—it could be catastrophic."

The urgency of their task hung in the air as they organized their resources, the note a silent testament to the looming threat. As they divided their tasks, with Leo focusing on operational logistics and Elise diving deeper into the esoteric analysis, the precinct buzzed around them, unaware of the potential danger brewing on the horizon. Their determination to prevent the ritual was more than professional duty; it was a race against an unseen and barely understood adversary, with stakes that were becoming alarmingly high.

In the dimly lit confines of an old coffee shop near the university, Elise Bennett and Leo Marquez sat across from a nervous-looking man in his late thirties, whose academic demeanor belied his current anxious state. Dr. Felix Armand, a historian specializing in esoteric cults and mythologies, had been identified as a potentially crucial informant. Despite his initial reluctance, the gravity of the situation had compelled him to agree to meet.

Dr. Armand sipped his coffee slowly, his eyes darting around the café before settling on the detectives. "I heard about what happened to Greaves," he began, his voice low. "And I know why you're here. I can't tell you everything—some of this is beyond what you'd consider... normal investigative parameters."

Elise leaned forward, her expression serious. "Dr. Armand, we understand there are sensitivities with the information you have, but we're dealing with potentially dangerous individuals. Anything you can share could be critical."

The historian adjusted his glasses, seeming to measure his words carefully. "The group you're interested in—The Order of the Ancestral Veil— they've been around for decades, but recently, there's been a shift in their activities. They believe in harnessing what they call 'primal energies' through rituals that are... well, they're not just symbolic."

Leo, his patience fraying, interjected softly, "We've seen evidence of their rituals. Victims, altars, symbols that suggest they're escalating."

Dr. Armand nodded, his fingers trembling slightly as he placed his cup down. "Yes, it's true. Their leader, whom they refer to only as 'The Guide', has been pushing them towards something big. They think the upcoming celestial alignment is a... a gateway. They're planning a major event, something they believe will grant them power, or insight, into realms beyond the typical understanding."

"And you think this event is what the ritual at the Wilson estate was preparing for?" Elise asked, piecing together his hints with their findings.

"Precisely," Dr. Armand confirmed. "The alignment they're obsessed with—it happens once every few centuries. In their belief system, it's a moment when the barriers between realities are thinnest. They want to exploit this."

Elise exchanged a glance with Leo, both understanding the severity of what Armand described. "Do you know where this event is supposed to take place?" she pressed.

Dr. Armand hesitated, glancing toward the window as if considering the cost of his next words. "I don't know the exact location, but it's somewhere north of here. They use coded language in their communications, but I've heard them mention 'the place where the stars meet the earth.' It's cryptic, but it's all I have."

"Thank you, Dr. Armand. This helps more than you might realize," Leo said, his tone appreciative yet urgent. "We'll do our best to prevent any harm they may intend."

As they stood to leave, Elise handed Dr. Armand her card. "If you think of anything else, or if you feel you're in danger, please call me immediately."

Dr. Armand nodded, his gaze lingering on the card before tucking it away securely. "I will. And... be careful. You're dealing with people who believe they have nothing to lose."

The detectives left the coffee shop, the weight of Dr. Armand's information settling over them like a heavy cloak. As they returned to their vehicle, the city around them felt eerily calm, a stark contrast to the storm they knew was brewing just beyond the visible horizon. Their next steps were clear, yet the path was shrouded in the murk of ancient beliefs and modern dangers, a combination that promised only uncertainty and shadows ahead.

Back at the precinct, Elise Bennett delved deeper into the tangled web of The Order of the Ancestral Veil, piecing together fragments of lore and whispers of dark practices that Dr. Felix Armand had hinted at. With each document she perused, each note she decoded, the gravity of their situation became starkly clearer. This was no mere gathering of misguided mystics; it was a network with tendrils deeply embedded in the cultural and historical substrata of their city.

The office was quiet, save for the steady hum of computers and the occasional murmur of distant conversations. Leo Marquez was at his desk, sorting through reports from their field agents and cross-referencing known associates of The Order with recent activities around the city.

"Elise, you should see this," Leo called out, his tone indicating he had stumbled upon something significant. He held up a map marked with various locations, each pinpointed with meticulous care. "The places marked here align with historical sites known for celestial observances. It seems The Order has been focusing on these sites, potentially as part of their ritual preparations."

Elise approached, her eyes scanning the map. "It fits with what Armand said about the celestial alignment. They're not just using random locations; these sites are chosen for their historical and astronomical significance."

She returned to her desk, pulling up a digital archive of esoteric texts that might shed light on the specific practices of The Order. The texts spoke of ancient rites meant to commune with celestial energies, practices believed to open gateways between worlds. The implications were chilling, and Elise felt a shiver run down her spine as she considered what such beliefs, when taken to extremes, could compel people to do.

"We need to anticipate their next move," she muttered, more to herself than to Leo. "If they believe this upcoming alignment is as significant as they claim, their next gathering could be catastrophic."

Leo nodded, his expression somber. "I've put out alerts to all units to keep an eye on the marked sites. We're also monitoring communications for any mention of The Order's activities. Whatever they're planning, we'll be ready."

Elise spent the next few hours compiling a detailed report on The Order's beliefs and rituals. It was a deep dive into a world where myth and reality blurred, where the boundaries of belief were pushed to dangerous extremes. The report outlined the potential psychological and sociological impacts of such beliefs, highlighting how they could manifest in illegal and harmful activities.

As the day turned into evening, the precinct grew quieter, the bustling energy of the daytime shift giving way to the more subdued tone of the night crew. Elise and Leo continued their work, each aware of the ticking clock as the celestial event approached.

Finally, Elise leaned back in her chair, her eyes tired from hours of intense focus. "We've done all we can for now," she said, her voice reflecting both determination and fatigue. "We've alerted the authorities, prepared our teams, and gathered as much intelligence as possible. Now, we wait and watch."

Leo stood, stretching his stiff muscles. "I hate waiting. Especially when we know something's coming."

"It's the hardest part," Elise agreed, packing up her things. "But we're not in the dark. We know what they believe, and we know where they might strike. We're as ready as we can be."

As they left the precinct, the city outside seemed almost normal, the everyday activities of its citizens continuing unabated. But beneath the veneer of normalcy, Elise and Leo moved with the knowledge that they were potentially days away from confronting a threat that sought to unravel the very fabric of reality. It was a heavy burden to carry into the quiet of the night.

In the strategic operations room of the precinct, the atmosphere was tense but focused. Maps of the city and its surrounding areas were spread across the walls, and digital screens displayed real-time data feeds from various surveillance points. Elise Bennett and Leo Marquez, along with a team of tactical planners and intelligence analysts, were gathered around a large table, reviewing the deployment strategy for the upcoming operation.

"The celestial alignment is in two days," Leo started, pointing to a calendar marked heavily with notes and times. "That's our window. According to everything we've gathered, that's when they'll attempt their ritual."

Elise, her eyes scanning the deployment charts, added, "Our best bet is to cover all known historical sites that align with the astronomical data and the locations identified in our intel from Dr. Armand. We need teams at each site, ready to move on my signal."

The room listened intently as she continued, "Surveillance will be critical. We'll use drones for overhead views and thermal imaging to detect any unusual gatherings. I want no blind spots."

A logistics officer chimed in, "We've coordinated with local law enforcement and the state police for additional support. All units will be on tactical standby. We've also briefed SWAT teams on the potential for ritualistic activity and what that might entail."

Leo looked over the maps, his finger tracing a route from the city center to the northern outskirts. "In addition to our physical presence, we need to monitor all communications coming in and out of these areas. If The Order suspects we're onto them, they might change locations at the last minute."

Elise nodded, her mind working through various scenarios. "Let's also set up checkpoints on all major routes leading to the primary sites. I don't want anyone slipping through our net."

The tactical team leader, a seasoned officer, reviewed the deployment details. "We'll have two teams for each site, one in stealth mode and one on immediate standby. Helicopters will be ready for quick deployment if we need to shift our focus."

As the meeting progressed, the team fine-tuned the plan, ensuring every possible contingency was covered. Communication protocols were set, emergency response procedures were reviewed, and roles were assigned with precision.

After the meeting concluded, the room slowly emptied, leaving Elise and Leo to gather their notes and prepare for the long hours ahead.

Leo paused, looking over the detailed plans covering the table. "You think we'll stop them in time?"

Elise, gathering her laptop and papers, responded with a measured tone. "We have to. There's too much at stake. This isn't just about preventing a crime; it's about protecting the reality as we know it."

They walked out of the operations room together, their steps echoing in the empty hallway. Outside, the sun was setting, casting long shadows across the city streets. The coming night brought with it a chill that seemed to seep into the bones, a reminder of the darkness they were racing against.

As they stepped into the cool evening air, their resolve was firm. The city around them continued its usual rhythm, unaware of the high stakes hidden beneath the calm surface. In the quiet before the storm, Elise and Leo were the watchful guardians, poised to confront whatever the night would bring.

Chapter 7
Inside The Order

The evening was cool and clear, a stark contrast to the tension brewing within the tactical operations tent pitched just outside the perimeter of their primary target location. The old observatory, a site known for its historical astronomical significance and recently flagged for unusual activities, was now the focus of a significant police operation. Elise Bennett and Leo Marquez reviewed the final details with their team, the air thick with anticipation.

Elise adjusted her bulletproof vest, checking her gear as she spoke to the assembled team. "This isn't just about arresting a few troublemakers; this is about stopping a potentially dangerous ritual. We need to be precise, silent, and quick. Remember, our goal is to prevent any harm they may intend."

Leo, double-checking his own equipment, added, "Surveillance has confirmed there are multiple individuals already on site, likely setting up. We have eyes in the sky and around the perimeter. Nothing goes unnoticed tonight."

A junior detective, part of the infiltration team, piped up, his voice slightly tense. "What's the signal for moving in?"

"We go on my command," Elise responded firmly. "If you see or hear anything before then that you think we should know about, report it immediately, but do not engage unless absolutely necessary."

The team leader for the SWAT unit, a large man with a calm demeanor, reviewed the entry strategy. "We'll approach from two sides. Alpha team will take the west approach through the woods for cover. Bravo team, you're with me on the east side. It's more exposed, but we'll use the terrain to our advantage."

Elise looked around at the faces of her team, each member ready but visibly carrying the weight of the operation's risks. "We've trained for this. We know what they're capable of, and we have the element of surprise. Stick to the plan, watch your partner's back, and stay alert."

Leo chimed in with a final piece of tactical advice. "Use your night vision gear until we're ready to breach. We need every advantage we can get."

As the briefing concluded, the team members began their final gear checks. Radios crackled with last-minute confirmations and status updates from the surveillance crew. The atmosphere was a blend of professional focus and underlying adrenaline as the teams prepared to move out.

Elise pulled Leo aside for a brief moment, her expression resolute. "Once we're in, keep communication open. I'll be relying on your updates to coordinate our moves inside."

Leo nodded, his response a reflection of their mutual trust and understanding. "I've got your back, Elise. We'll get them tonight."

With a final nod to her team, Elise led the way out of the tent. They moved silently in the growing darkness towards their designated positions, the night air carrying the distant sounds of the woodland that surrounded the observatory.

As they advanced, the old structure loomed ahead, its silhouette a ghostly presence against the night sky. It was an eerie sight, the once-grand observatory now a focal point for clandestine activities far removed from its original purpose.

Each team member's breath seemed loud in their ears, a stark reminder of the quiet surrounding them, punctuated only by the soft sounds of their careful steps. As they neared their entry points, the command to halt was given, and each person took a moment to steady themselves, knowing that the operation's success depended on what would happen in the next few hours.

In the shadows of the night, Elise and her team waited for the go-ahead, each second ticking by with agonizing slowness. They were not just law enforcement tonight; they were the thin line between order and chaos, ready to face whatever lay within the walls of the old observatory.

The old observatory, now a hub of clandestine activity, was alive with the hushed murmur of robed figures as they prepared for their ceremony. Hidden in the shadows, Elise Bennett and her team observed the gathering through night vision lenses, their presence undetected. The large, domed room of the observatory, once used for stargazing, had been transformed into a ritualistic chamber, marked with symbols and candles arranged in an intricate pattern on the floor.

Elise, positioned behind a dilapidated wall with Leo Marquez and two other officers, whispered into her radio, "Visual confirmation on at least twenty individuals, all robed. The central figure is likely the leader—'The Guide' they refer to."

Leo, watching through his binoculars, added, "No sign of hostages or outsiders. Looks like this is their core group. Any indication of the ritual starting?"

"Not yet," Elise replied, her voice low. "They seem to be waiting for something—or someone. The alignment isn't for another hour."

The soft glow of the moonlight filtering through the observatory's open dome provided just enough light for the eerie scene to unfold with cinematic surrealism. The figures moved with purpose, each action deliberate, contributing to the preparations of what was clearly an event of significant importance to them.

"The place is secured?" Elise asked, double-checking their operational readiness.

"Alpha and Bravo are in position, no movements outside the planned entry points. We're tight here," confirmed Leo, his focus never wavering from the scene before them.

As they watched, a latecomer, also robed, hurried into the gathering, carrying a small, ancient-looking chest. The central figure, 'The Guide,' received it with ceremonial gravity, placing it near the center of the formation. The crowd's attention was riveted on the chest as 'The Guide' began to speak, though his words were inaudible from their position.

"They're starting," Elise noted, her hand instinctively moving to her sidearm. "We wait for my signal. Once they begin, we move in during the distraction. We need to control the situation before it escalates."

Leo nodded, passing on the orders quietly through his radio. The tension among the team was palpable; each member was aware that the timing of their intervention was critical. Too early, and they might provoke a standoff. Too late, and the ritual could reach a point they were desperate to avoid.

Minutes passed like hours as the gathering's intensity grew. Chants in a strange language began to fill the space, rising and falling with a rhythm that was unsettling in its fervency. Elise glanced at Leo, her eyes communicating her concern. They were both experienced enough to know that situations like these could spiral out of control quickly.

Finally, 'The Guide' raised his hands, signaling the commencement of the main part of the ritual. As he opened the chest, revealing its contents—a collection of ancient artifacts and manuscripts—the team braced for action.

"Now," Elise whispered, her voice calm yet commanding. "Go!"

In a coordinated rush, police officers broke from cover, storming the observatory with precision. Commands to halt and drop to the ground echoed through the chamber, startling the gathered members of The

Order. Confusion and panic set in among the robed figures as they were quickly subdued and handcuffed by the officers.

Leo led a group to secure 'The Guide,' who, despite the chaos, seemed resigned to his fate. Elise directed another team to gather all ritualistic items as evidence.

As the observatory's dome above reflected the chaos below, the night's silence was shattered by the reality of the law reclaiming order from the clutches of those who sought to bend it to their arcane will.

In the aftermath of the raid, Elise Bennett and Leo Marquez found themselves in a small, stark interrogation room across from the subdued figure of 'The Guide,' real name Marcus Eldridge. He sat quietly, his hands cuffed in front of him, a calm demeanor belying the gravity of his situation.

Elise began, her tone professional yet probing, "Mr. Eldridge, you understand why you're here. We interrupted what we believe was a very dangerous event. I'd like to understand more about what you were trying to accomplish."

Marcus looked up, his eyes clear and unnervingly calm. "Detective Bennett, I'm aware of how our actions might appear to outsiders. But our goals are purely spiritual. We seek to open the pathways of understanding—between the seen and the unseen."

Leo interjected, his skepticism palpable, "By conducting rituals that involve illegal activities? There were families worried sick about some of your... followers."

"The path to enlightenment isn't always understood by those not walking it," Marcus replied smoothly. "Everyone present tonight came willingly. They seek what we all seek—knowledge beyond what is readily available."

Elise leaned forward slightly, pressing him, "Knowledge that involves illegal activities? We have evidence of harm coming to those involved with your group. How do you justify that?"

Marcus sighed, a hint of frustration crossing his features. "There is always risk in transformation. The caterpillar does not become a butterfly without struggle."

"But we're not talking about insects, Mr. Eldridge, we're talking about human lives," Elise countered sharply. "People who were hurt, families torn apart by your so-called transformation."

Leo picked up the thread, his tone harder, "We need specifics about your plans for tonight. What was the ultimate goal of this ritual?"

Marcus looked between them, then down at his hands before responding. "The alignment tonight was an auspicious time, a rare moment when the barriers thin. We intended to reach through these veils to draw forth knowledge, to commune with energies that are ancient and wise."

"And what cost was acceptable for this communion? What were you willing to sacrifice?" Elise asked, her gaze steady.

Marcus met her eyes, his own reflecting a depth of belief that was almost disconcerting. "All great advancements require sacrifice. Our members understand this."

"That doesn't give you the right to decide for them, especially when it crosses into illegality," Leo said, his voice firm. "You were playing with people's lives, Marcus. That's not a spiritual pursuit; that's manipulation."

Marcus's expression tightened, then relaxed. "I see we will not agree on the nature of my actions. I believe deeply in our work, as do my followers."

Elise noted this, her mind already cataloging his responses for further investigation. "We will be speaking with your followers, Mr. Eldridge. And if we find evidence of coercion or any harm coming from your actions, you will be held accountable."

Marcus nodded solemnly, "I understand, Detective. And I will cooperate with your investigation within the boundaries of my beliefs."

As they concluded the interview, Elise and Leo stepped out into the corridor, the heavy door closing with a thud behind them.

Leo shook his head, his expression troubled. "Think he believes his own rhetoric?"

"He does," Elise responded, her voice thoughtful. "That's what makes him dangerous. He's not just a leader; he's a believer."

As they walked towards the exit, the weight of the conversation lingered, a reminder of the complex interplay between belief and law, and the fine line they treaded in protecting one from the other. Their work was far from over, but tonight, they had prevented something potentially catastrophic, and that was a victory, albeit a somber one.

After wrapping up at the precinct, Elise Bennett and Leo Marquez decided to revisit the observatory one last time to ensure no evidence was overlooked in the chaos of the raid. The night was deep and quiet, a stark contrast to the earlier adrenaline-filled hours. As they approached the now-secured building, the scene was calm, with police tape fluttering gently in the night breeze.

As they entered the main hall of the observatory, their flashlights cut through the darkness, casting long shadows across the walls. The remnants of the disrupted ritual lay scattered, a silent testament to the night's events.

Leo paused, examining a piece of cloth on the ground. "Looks like part of a robe. Must've been torn during the scuffle."

Elise nodded, her mind still on their earlier conversation with Marcus Eldridge. "He's deep in his beliefs. Convincing him of the harm caused by his actions is going to be tough."

As they continued their sweep, a noise from the upper gallery caught their attention. Elise signaled to Leo, and they quietly ascended the stairs, their hands resting on their holstered guns. At the top, they found a small, hidden alcove overlooking the main hall. Inside, crouched and seemingly hiding, was a young woman, her face pale and eyes wide with fear.

"Don't shoot!" she exclaimed, her voice trembling. "I'm not one of them. I—I was hiding."

Elise stepped forward, her flashlight illuminating the woman's face. "It's okay, you're safe now. Can you tell us your name and what you're doing here?"

"My name is Julia," she replied, her voice steadying slightly as she looked up at the detectives. "I came here with them, but I couldn't go through with it. I didn't believe in... in what they wanted to do."

Leo, keeping his voice calm, asked, "What were they planning, Julia? Can you tell us anything that might help?"

Julia nodded, pulling her knees closer to her chest. "They talked about opening a gateway, about powers from another place. I thought it was just philosophical, but then I saw them bringing in... items, and the way they prepared tonight, I got scared."

Elise crouched down to be at eye level with Julia. "What kind of items? Anything specific you can remember might be very helpful."

"They had old manuscripts, stones, and some very old artifacts. Marcus said they were keys to the gateway. I didn't see much; I ran up here when everyone started gathering."

"Did you see anything else, any plans for after tonight?" Leo inquired, taking notes.

Julia shook her head. "No, I just knew I had to get away. But I heard them mention a fallback location, somewhere they would regroup if things went wrong. It's a house in the woods, north of here. That's all I know."

"That's very helpful, Julia. Thank you," Elise said, standing up. "You did the right thing by not participating. We'll need to take you in for a statement, and then we can ensure you're safe."

As they escorted Julia down to their vehicle, the night seemed to close in around them, the gravity of the situation settling deeper. The observatory, a place meant for looking outward to the stars, had been turned inward to darker pursuits. Elise and Leo exchanged a look, both understanding the importance of Julia's information.

The drive back was quiet, each lost in thought. The encounter with Julia had opened a new lead, pointing to deeper layers of The Order's plans. As they neared the precinct, the first light of dawn was breaking, casting a new light on the city they were sworn to protect. It was a reminder that their work, like the day, was just beginning.

Chapter 8
A Tense Alliance

As dawn broke over the city, the light filtering through the blinds cast long shadows across the conference room where Elise Bennett and Leo Marquez gathered with their team for a critical debriefing. The room was abuzz with activity as officers and specialists prepped for the session, laying out documents and queuing up presentations that detailed the previous night's events and findings.

The debriefing began with Elise summarizing the operation's outcomes, her tone professional but underscored with urgency. "Last night, we successfully disrupted what could have been a significant event for The Order of the Ancestral Veil. Thanks to actionable intelligence and coordinated efforts, no lives were lost, and multiple members of the group are now in custody, including their leader, Marcus Eldridge."

Leo then took over, focusing on the operational challenges they faced. "Our approach was stealthy and precise, but this group was prepared, more than we anticipated. Their readiness indicates they might have been tipped off, or they are just more cautious due to past disruptions. We need to consider this in our future strategies."

The room nodded in agreement, the weight of the operation's complexity settling in. One of the intelligence analysts stood, clicking forward a slide showing maps and photographs of the observatory and other related sites. "We've secured several items that were clearly intended for use in their ritual—artifacts, manuscripts, and other paraphernalia. Preliminary assessments suggest these are not just historical curiosities; some may be genuinely dangerous if used in the intended manner."

As the briefing continued, discussions turned toward the implications of their findings. Elise interjected, highlighting the broader context. "We need to understand not just the 'how' but the 'why' behind their actions.

Their belief system drives them, and if we're to prevent future incidents, we must disrupt their narrative, not just their ceremonies."

A senior tactical advisor raised a point of concern. "We also need to consider the potential for backlash or retaliatory actions from other members of The Order not yet identified. Their network may be larger than the individuals captured last night."

Elise acknowledged this with a nod. "Correct. We're dealing with an ideology, not just an isolated group. Our response should be multidimensional—legal, psychological, and community-based."

The meeting then shifted to discuss the next steps. Leo outlined the immediate action items. "First, we continue processing and interrogating the detainees to extract more information about further planned activities. Second, we step up our surveillance and intelligence-gathering efforts, particularly focusing on any communication leaks that could suggest how they knew we were coming."

Finally, as the team began to disperse, tasked with their various assignments, Elise and Leo lingered behind, contemplating the challenges ahead. The morning's debrief had crystallized the scale of the threat posed by The Order, but it also sharpened their resolve.

As the room emptied, Elise turned to Leo, her expression serious but determined. "We're in for a long battle, Leo. One that's as much about ideas as it is about the law."

Leo agreed, his voice resolute. "And it's a battle we need to win, Elise. For the safety of the city and the integrity of our societal values."

Together, they left the conference room, stepping out into the bustling precinct, ready to tackle the next phase of their investigation. The challenges were significant, but so was their commitment to safeguarding their community against the dark ambitions of The Order.

The task of garnering support from various law enforcement and community sectors was both critical and challenging. Elise Bennett and Leo Marquez found themselves in the municipal building, preparing to meet with city officials, local leaders, and representatives from various community organizations. Their goal was clear: to establish a robust network of support and information-sharing that could help prevent the type of incidents orchestrated by The Order of the Ancestral Veil.

As they entered the large conference room, the buzz of conversation tapered off, and all eyes turned towards them. They took their places at the front, ready to make their case.

Leo opened the meeting. "Thank you all for coming on such short notice. We're here because we need a united front against a threat that has shown it doesn't respect the bounds of law and morality. The Order of the Ancestral Veil isn't just a criminal group; it's a cult with deep roots and dangerous intentions."

Elise continued, "Our recent operations have uncovered just how far they're willing to go. We've seen evidence of rituals meant to harness what they believe are supernatural forces, which clearly cross into illegal activities, including endangerment and possible coercion."

A city council member leaned forward, her expression concerned. "What exactly are you asking from us? How can we help when this seems... well, out of our league?"

Elise nodded, understanding the hesitance. "We're not just asking for enforcement support. We need educational programs that can inform the public about the dangers of such cults. We need community leaders like yourselves to help identify and support individuals who may be vulnerable to recruitment by such groups."

A representative from a local community center raised his hand, asking, "Are there specific signs we should look for in individuals who might be getting involved with The Order?"

"Yes," Leo answered, projecting a slide with bullet points. "Changes in behavior, sudden secrecy, new affiliations with known members, unusual interest in specific historical or astronomical events, among others. Our team can provide training sessions and workshops."

Another hand went up, this time from the head of a local neighborhood watch program. "Can you provide us with materials or information that we can distribute in our communities? Flyers, posters, things like that?"

"Absolutely," Elise replied, jotting down a note. "We'll provide you with all the materials you need. Education is just as powerful a tool as enforcement in this case."

The police chief, who had been listening intently, finally spoke. "We'll also need to increase patrols and surveillance in key areas, especially around historical sites and during astronomical events that The Order might consider significant. I'll coordinate with other agencies to ensure we have coverage."

A local school superintendent suggested, "Perhaps we could incorporate discussions about the dangers of cults into our social studies or history curricula?"

"That's an excellent idea," Elise agreed, pleased with the proactive suggestion. "Awareness can prevent recruitment and can empower our youth to make informed choices."

As the meeting progressed, more ideas were exchanged, from hosting community forums to setting up a hotline for tips about suspicious activities. The atmosphere in the room shifted from cautious concern to proactive planning, each participant eager to contribute to the new strategy against The Order.

By the end of the session, Elise and Leo had not only presented their case but had also ignited a collective response that promised broader civic engagement. They thanked everyone for their contributions and commitment as the meeting adjourned.

As they left the municipal building, Leo looked at Elise, a faint smile breaking through the exhaustion. "That went better than I expected. Feels good to have the city behind us."

"It does," Elise acknowledged, feeling a renewed sense of hope. "But the real work starts now. Let's make sure this alliance holds strong."

The evening closed on a note of cautious optimism, with the city united in its stance against a hidden enemy. The challenge was daunting, yet the newly forged alliance brought with it a stronger front ready to face whatever The Order might attempt next.

Later that day, back at the precinct, Elise Bennett and Leo Marquez convened with their core investigative team to refine their approach based on the alliance they had forged earlier. The meeting room was filled with the low hum of serious conversation as the team prepared to integrate community resources into their operational strategy.

Leo, standing by a whiteboard filled with notes and diagrams, addressed the team. "We've got the city's backing now, which is great. But that doesn't mean we can relax. Skepticism about our ability to handle this situation is high. We need to be on top of our game, more than ever."

Elise chimed in, her tone pragmatic as she distributed copies of the community engagement plan. "Yes, and it's vital we address any skepticism head-on by being transparent with our operations where we can, and always following up on our commitments. We've promised a lot, and now we must deliver."

Detective Harris, a seasoned member of the team, raised a concern. "There's a lot of talk about community involvement, which is good and all, but how do we ensure that this doesn't compromise our operational security? We're dealing with a group that's already proven they're watching us as closely as we're watching them."

"That's a valid point," Leo acknowledged, marking a section on the whiteboard labeled 'Security Measures.' "Part of our strategy needs to include strict information protocols. Only share what's necessary and keep the crucial details within this room."

Elise added, "We also need to set up regular check-ins with all our community contacts. If they see something, they say something. It goes both ways—we inform them of potential risks, and they keep us in the loop on the ground chatter."

A junior analyst, part of the team responsible for monitoring communications, interjected, "We've enhanced our surveillance and data collection techniques, especially around known hotspots and during key astronomical events The Order might be interested in. But we should also consider misinformation—deliberately leaking false operation details to see if they surface in our intercepts."

"That's an excellent tactic," Elise noted, writing it down under 'Countermeasures.' "It could help us identify any leaks or spies within our network or among our new alliances."

Leo nodded in agreement, then turned his attention to integrating the educational programs into their strategy. "We need these educational initiatives to start rolling out as soon as possible. The more informed the public is, the harder it will be for The Order to operate in the shadows."

"I'll coordinate with the community leaders and set up a schedule for workshops and seminars," offered Detective Martinez, who had been quiet, listening and taking notes. "I think starting with schools and local community centers will cast the widest net."

"Good," Elise said with a nod. "And let's not forget the importance of online engagement. A lot of recruitment and information sharing happens over the internet. We need a strong digital presence."

As the meeting drew to a close, Leo summarized their collective responsibility. "Everyone here has a role to play. This isn't just about stopping bad things from happening; it's about protecting our community's way of life. Let's make sure we're proactive, not just reactive."

The team dispersed, each member clear on their duties and the high stakes involved. As Elise and Leo collected their papers and prepared to leave, they shared a brief, knowing look—a mutual acknowledgment of the challenges ahead, tempered by the resolve to meet them head-on.

The night outside was settling in as they left the precinct, the darkness a reminder of the shadowy nature of their adversaries. But armed with a solid strategy and a united front, they were ready to shine a light into those dark corners and protect their city.

As dusk settled over the city, casting long shadows across the streets, Elise Bennett and Leo Marquez were back at the precinct, poring over recent surveillance footage that had just come in. The day's meetings had strengthened their external alliances, but the real work continued behind the scenes where every lead, every piece of evidence, could be the key to dismantling The Order of the Ancestral Veil from within.

In a small, cluttered office, the glow from multiple monitors lit up their faces as they reviewed the digital feeds. One particular video, captured from a hidden camera near a known Order meeting spot, showed a figure handing off a suspicious package to another cloaked individual. The exchange was quick, almost missed among the typical evening bustle, but to the trained eye, it stood out as a potential lead.

"Rewind that," Elise instructed, leaning closer to the screen. Leo obliged, playing back the footage slowly. "There. Pause." The screen froze on the face of the individual receiving the package, partially obscured but possibly recognizable.

"I think that's one of the lower-ranking members we've had under surveillance," Leo noted, squinting at the screen. "Goes by the name of Derek Simms."

Elise nodded, pulling up a file on her laptop. "Simms has been on the radar for a while but never as anything more than a peripheral figure. This could indicate he's more involved than we thought."

The implications were significant. If Simms was moving up in the ranks, or if he was part of a splinter group within The Order, it could lead them to new information about the organization's structure or future plans.

"We need to bring him in," Leo decided, already reaching for his phone to coordinate with their field team. "Quietly. No alarms, no scenes."

Elise agreed, her mind racing through the next steps. "Once we have him, we'll need to work quickly. He might not know much, but whatever he does know could be time-sensitive."

As Leo communicated with the field team, Elise drafted the necessary paperwork to bring Simms in for questioning. Their office, usually a place of strategizing and planning, had turned into a command center, buzzing with the urgency of the hunt.

Hours later, news came through that Simms had been picked up without incident and was on his way to the precinct. Elise and Leo prepared for the interrogation, each aware that this could be a turning point in their investigation.

When Simms arrived, he was escorted into an interrogation room, a nondescript space designed to focus attention solely on the conversation at hand. Elise and Leo entered, their expressions neutral but firm.

"Derek, you're not in here because we think you're the mastermind," Elise began, her tone straightforward but not accusing. "But you've been caught in something that's bigger than you might realize. We can help you, but you need to help us first."

Simms, visibly nervous, shifted in his seat but remained silent.

Leo leaned forward slightly, his approach slightly softer. "Look, Derek, we know you're not at the top of this... organization. But whatever you were doing tonight, whatever that package contained, it's important. Tell us what it was, and maybe we can sort things out in a way that benefits everyone."

The room fell silent as Simms considered his options. Outside, the precinct buzzed softly, a reminder of the world moving forward, relentless and indifferent to the dramas unfolding within its walls.

Finally, Simms spoke, his voice a mixture of resignation and relief. "It was documents," he admitted. "Plans for... I don't know exactly. They don't tell me everything."

"Documents about what?" Elise pressed gently.

"Locations. Rituals. Some new places they're interested in," Simms divulged, looking down at his hands.

Elise and Leo exchanged a glance, both recognizing the importance of this information. They ended the interrogation with a promise to Simms that they would do what they could to keep him safe, provided he cooperated fully.

As they stepped out of the interrogation room, the night had deepened, the darkness outside mirroring the dark revelations of the evening. But with each piece of the puzzle that fell into place, the path forward cleared slightly, guiding them through the shadows toward the light of understanding and resolution.

Chapter 9
Third Murder

Under the cloak of night, Elise Bennett and Leo Marquez coordinated a meticulous setup of surveillance equipment around a suspected new location of The Order's activity. This area, an old, abandoned factory on the outskirts of the city, had been identified from the documents Derek Simms had provided during his interrogation.

The factory was secluded, surrounded by dense woods, providing ample cover for the team as they approached. Elise, equipped with night vision goggles, scanned the perimeter while speaking softly into her radio. "Team two, position your cameras to cover the south entrance. We need eyes on all possible exit points."

Leo, overseeing the placement of motion sensors along the fence line, responded, "Got it, Elise. Team three, how are we looking on the east side?"

"East side is clear, setting up the last of the cameras now," came the crisp reply over the radio.

The operation was tense, with every team member aware of the potential dangers. The factory was large, with multiple entries and shadowed corners that could hide unwanted surprises.

As they regrouped near the command vehicle, a mobile unit equipped with monitors displaying feeds from the installed cameras, Leo reviewed the setup. "Let's run a check on all camera feeds. I want to make sure we're not blind on any angle."

Elise nodded, her attention fixed on a monitor showing the live feed from a thermal imaging camera. "There's some heat signatures inside, could be our suspects, or it could be wildlife. Let's keep monitoring."

A technician at the controls zoomed in on the area Elise was observing. "I'll keep an eye on these signatures, see if there's any pattern or movement that suggests human activity."

"Good," Elise affirmed, then turned to address a group of officers preparing for potential entry. "Remember, if we go in, it needs to be fast and silent. No surprises. We can't afford a misstep, not with what's at stake."

Leo, checking his watch, added, "We'll give it another hour on surveillance. If we see definitive human activity, we move in. If not, we hold until daylight. Either way, we maintain stealth. This isn't just about catching them; it's about catching them unaware."

As the team members nodded and went back to their posts, the tension was palpable, but so was the determination. Each officer understood their role and the importance of their tasks.

The hour passed slowly, with occasional updates from the surveillance teams. Elise and Leo used this time to discuss further strategies. "If this is their new base, it could be where they're planning to regroup after tonight's disruption," Elise theorized, her eyes never leaving the monitors.

Leo agreed, his voice low and steady. "Which means they could be planning something bigger. We've already seen what they're capable of. We can't let them regroup or gain momentum."

Finally, a clear pattern emerged from the heat signatures inside the factory. The technician adjusted the focus, confirming their suspicions. "Definite human movement, seems structured, not random. Looks like at least four individuals."

Elise made the call. "That's our cue. Leo, take point with team one. I'll coordinate from here and follow in with team two."

With precision and a well-practiced calm, Leo led the first team towards the factory, moving through the shadows to approach the main entrance.

Elise watched the monitors intently, each screen a portal to the unfolding operation, her hand poised over the radio, ready to issue commands or provide support as needed.

As the teams moved in, the factory's silent, looming presence seemed to await them, a sentinel to secrets yet uncovered. The night deepened around them, a backdrop to the high stakes of their endeavor, each step forward a careful balance between caution and urgency.

Inside the old factory, the air was thick with dust and decay, the echo of the team's footsteps a stark contrast to the silence that pervaded the structure. Leo Marquez led his team with caution, their flashlights cutting through the darkness, revealing the aged machinery and scattered debris of a long-abandoned place.

As they advanced, Leo's radio crackled softly, Elise Bennett's voice steady in his ear. "Visual confirmation from exterior cams. You have two moving towards the north end of the main floor. Proceed with caution."

Acknowledging with a quiet "Roger that," Leo signaled his team to adjust their approach, moving towards the north end while maintaining a tight formation. The beams from their flashlights occasionally flickered across walls covered in graffiti and old posters, remnants of the factory's past life.

The grim ambiance was suddenly pierced by a soft murmur of voices, prompting the team to halt. Leo gestured for silence, and they listened. The voices were muffled, the words indistinct, but the tone was urgent. Creeping closer, they reached a makeshift barrier of crates and old furniture that sectioned off part of the area.

Leo peered around the edge, his hand signaling his team to prepare for a potential confrontation. What he saw made him pause—a small group of individuals huddled around something on the floor. It wasn't a planning session; it was another ritual, but this one had clearly gone awry. Amid the group lay a figure, still and lifeless, with others kneeling around in apparent dismay.

Taking a deep breath, Leo stepped out, his authoritative voice breaking the tense silence. "Police! Everyone step away from the body and put your hands where I can see them!"

The group scattered in panic, but the officers were quick to respond, detaining the individuals before they could flee the scene. As the rest of the team secured the suspects, Leo approached the body, his flashlight revealing a young man, his face ashen, eyes wide open in a frozen gaze of fear.

Elise arrived moments later, her expression grim as she assessed the scene. "What happened here?" she asked, kneeling beside the body to check for signs of life, though it was clear the man was beyond help.

"It looks like another ritual, but something went wrong," Leo reported, watching as the forensic team began to set up around them.

Elise glanced around at the detained individuals, their faces a mixture of fear and shock. "We need to find out if this was intended or an accident. Either way, it's another life lost to this madness."

As the forensic team worked, Elise and Leo interviewed the detained individuals one by one. Their stories were fragmented, tinged with fear and confusion, but a picture gradually emerged of a ritual intended to empower one of their members, which had tragically backfired.

One of the younger members, a girl barely in her twenties, sobbed as she spoke. "It was supposed to be safe. Just a ritual to bless him, to give him strength. We didn't think it would... we didn't know..."

Elise took notes, her face a mask of professional neutrality, but her eyes betrayed her frustration. "Who led the ritual? Was it planned by Marcus Eldridge?"

"No, he... he wasn't here tonight. This was just us, trying to... to continue his work," the girl managed between sobs.

As the interviews concluded, Elise and Leo reconvened, their discussion low and urgent. "We're seeing the fallout of Eldridge's influence," Elise said, her voice tight with anger. "Even without him, they're continuing these dangerous rituals."

Leo nodded, his expression somber. "We need to tighten our grip on this group. This can't happen again. We'll start with the ones we've picked up tonight and work our way through the entire network."

As they exited the factory, the early morning light was beginning to creep across the sky, casting long shadows and illuminating the grim reality of their ongoing battle against a darkness that seemed to seep deeper into the city's fabric with each passing day.

After securing the perimeter of the old factory and ensuring all suspects were detained, Elise Bennett and Leo Marquez began a thorough investigation of the crime scene. The forensic team had already cordoned off the area around the body, and the dim light of early morning filtered through the broken windows, casting eerie shadows across the floor.

Elise crouched near the body, examining the scene while speaking to the forensic lead, Dr. Simmons. "What's the preliminary cause of death?" she asked, her voice low but clear.

Dr. Simmons, adjusting his glasses, responded carefully. "No obvious signs of trauma. It looks like it could be a cardiac event, but we'll need an autopsy to confirm. The setting and circumstances suggest it could have been induced by stress or other external factors."

Leo, who was examining some of the ritualistic paraphernalia scattered around, added, "These items, were they part of the ritual that went wrong?"

"Yes," Dr. Simmons replied, pointing to a series of symbols drawn around the body. "These symbols are similar to those we found in other locations used by The Order. They seem to be trying to channel some form of energy, at least that's their belief."

Elise stood, her attention now on the symbols. "Have we documented these patterns? They might give us more insight into what they were attempting."

"We have," a technician nearby answered, holding up a camera. "I've taken high-resolution images of the entire area. We'll analyze them back at the lab and cross-reference with the database of known occult symbols."

Leo walked over to a small table set aside from the main ritual area, where several open books lay alongside modern electronic devices. "It looks like they were mixing old and new methods. Here, there's a laptop logged into what seems to be a forum for occult enthusiasts."

Elise joined him, peering at the screen. "Can we trace any of their communications from that machine?"

"I've called in our tech team to handle this," Leo said, stepping back as a specialist approached to take over the laptop. "They'll do a deep dive into the files and online activity."

As they continued their examination, Elise's radio crackled to life. "Bennett, we've got something," came a voice from one of the teams searching the outer buildings.

"What is it?" Elise responded, her hand reaching automatically to adjust the volume.

"We found a stash of what looks like personal belongings—IDs, wallets, personal effects. It looks like they might belong to people who attended past gatherings. Some are reported missing."

"That's a significant find," Leo remarked, his brow furrowing. "It could help us identify more victims or people who might still be at risk."

"Collect everything," Elise instructed into the radio. "Document it meticulously. We'll need to contact families and follow up on each one."

The morning progressed with more discoveries, each piece adding to the complex puzzle of The Order's activities. As the investigation unfolded, the factory revealed more about the grim reality of what had been happening under the guise of spiritual rituals.

"Every piece we uncover shows just how deep this goes," Elise said to Leo as they prepared to leave the scene. "It's not just about misguided beliefs; it's manipulation on a large scale."

Leo nodded, his expression somber as he looked over the notes he had taken. "And it's our job to put an end to it. Let's make sure we use everything we've found here to build a strong case against them."

As they walked back to their vehicle, the early morning light had fully broken, casting long, sharp shadows behind them. The factory, now quiet and still, stood as a somber reminder of the night's events—a place where the search for truth had revealed the depths of human folly and manipulation.

As the sun crested higher in the sky, casting a stark light over the city, Elise Bennett and Leo Marquez returned to the precinct, their minds heavy with the morning's discoveries. The factory's grim secrets had provided substantial evidence, but also a sobering reminder of the dangers lurking beneath the surface of seemingly benign gatherings.

Inside the precinct, the atmosphere was tense as they prepared to interrogate one of the key suspects detained from the factory. This suspect, known only by the alias "Raven," was believed to be a primary organizer for The Order's more covert activities. The interrogation room was stark, a simple table and two chairs under harsh fluorescent lighting, designed to focus attention solely on the conversation at hand.

Elise took the lead, her approach methodical and direct. "We know you were instrumental in planning last night's event. What was the purpose of the ritual?"

Raven, a middle-aged man with sharp features, remained silent for a long moment before responding, his voice low. "Transformation. We seek to transform the world. To open minds to possibilities beyond your understanding."

Leo, standing by the door, added his voice to the questioning. "By putting people's lives at risk? We found a body, Raven. Someone died because of your 'transformation.'"

Raven's gaze flickered, a brief sign of disturbance crossing his otherwise composed demeanor. "A regrettable loss," he finally said, his tone still measured. "But evolution always comes at a cost."

Elise pressed on, not satisfied with the dismissive response. "Who else is involved? We know this goes beyond a handful of local gatherings."

Raven smirked slightly, leaning back. "The world is waking up, Detectives. You can't stop the dawn."

The interrogation continued, but Raven offered little in the way of concrete information, his answers a blend of evasion and cryptic philosophizing. Frustrated but undeterred, Elise and Leo concluded the session, aware that breaking through The Order's indoctrination would require more than direct questioning.

Afterward, Elise and Leo sat in her office, the blinds drawn against the glare of the afternoon sun, reflecting on the case's complexities. "It's like grappling with shadows," Elise remarked, her voice tinged with fatigue. "Every answer we uncover just leads to more questions."

Leo nodded, his expression thoughtful. "And every layer we peel back reveals more about how deep this goes. It's more than crime; it's a belief system that's deeply rooted in its followers."

"That's what makes it so dangerous," Elise agreed, leaning back in her chair. "It's not just the acts themselves but the ideology behind them. It spreads... infects."

The room was quiet for a moment, the only sound the distant hum of the precinct around them. Then Leo spoke up, his tone resolute. "We'll keep pulling at those threads, though. No matter how deep we have to go, we'll find a way to stop them."

Elise smiled faintly, appreciative of Leo's unwavering resolve. "That's all we can do. Stay the course and protect as many people as we can along the way."

As the day wound down, the precinct began to quiet, and Elise and Leo prepared to leave. They stepped out into the cooling evening, the sky a tapestry of orange and purple as the sun set on another day. The city around them buzzed with the life of its inhabitants, most unaware of the battles being fought in the shadows on their behalf.

Elise looked over at Leo, a partner not just in duty but in belief—the belief that their fight was worthwhile, that despite the darkness they faced, there was light worth fighting for. Together, they walked down the steps of the precinct, ready for whatever the next day would bring.

Chapter 10
Race Against Time

In the bustling heart of the precinct's forensic lab, Elise Bennett and Leo Marquez were deep in discussion with Dr. Simmons, the lead forensic analyst. They were surrounded by a flurry of activity as technicians processed the latest batch of evidence gathered from the raid at the old factory.

"Dr. Simmons, what have we got from the items recovered at the factory?" Elise asked, her eyes scanning over the array of evidence bags laid out on the lab table.

Dr. Simmons adjusted his glasses, picking up one of the bags containing a series of intricately carved stones. "These stones you found are not just decorative; they're historical artifacts, possibly ancient amulets. Their inscriptions are in a language that isn't immediately recognizable. We're consulting with a specialist in ancient languages to decode the text."

Leo leaned in, examining the stones through the bag. "Could understanding these inscriptions tell us more about The Order's intentions?"

"It's highly possible," Dr. Simmons replied. "Symbols and language like this are often used in rituals believed to hold power. Deciphering them could give us insight into their next move."

Elise turned her attention to another item, a book with worn leather binding and pages filled with notes and diagrams. "And this journal? Anything useful?"

Dr. Simmons nodded, handing her a sheet of paper. "We've transcribed several pages. The writer mentions a location repeatedly, referred to as the 'Sanctuary of Stars.' It's described almost like a holy site for them."

"Have we identified where this 'Sanctuary of Stars' could be?" Leo asked, his tone urgent.

"Not yet," Dr. Simmons admitted. "The descriptions are cryptic, but we've cross-referenced them with known historical sites in the area. We're narrowing down the possibilities."

Elise mulled over this information, tapping the table thoughtfully. "Keep pushing on that, Dr. Simmons. If we can find this sanctuary, it might be the key to preventing whatever they're planning next."

"Absolutely, I'll update you the moment we have something concrete," Dr. Simmons assured her, then turned to address a technician entering the lab with a box of electronic devices.

Leo picked up one of the devices, a hard drive. "What about the digital evidence? Any luck breaking into their data?"

"The tech team is still working on it, but they've managed to bypass the initial security on some of the drives," Dr. Simmons explained, gesturing towards the tech area where several computers were running data recovery processes. "We might have more to go on soon."

Elise nodded, her gaze fixed on the ongoing work. "Every piece of this puzzle is crucial. We're not just dealing with a criminal group; it's almost like a cult, with a belief system that motivates them to go to extremes."

Leo agreed, his expression serious. "And that makes them unpredictable and dangerous. We need to stay one step ahead."

As they continued to discuss the evidence, a technician approached, a printout in hand. "Dr. Simmons, we've got something from the hard drives. Looks like encrypted messages between members of The Order. We're decrypting them now, but it looks promising."

"Good work," Dr. Simmons responded, taking the printout and quickly scanning the content. "This could be what we need to piece together their plan."

Elise took the printout, her eyes quickly moving over the text. "Keep at it, everyone. Anything you find, no matter how small it might seem, report it immediately."

As they wrapped up in the lab, Elise and Leo left with a sense of cautious optimism. The race against time was intensifying, but with each new clue, they were closing in on The Order, piece by piece, ready to thwart their dark ambitions before more lives could be endangered.

In the secure confines of the strategy room, Elise Bennett and Leo Marquez convened with their top tactical team. The walls were lined with digital maps and screens showing live feeds from various surveillance points. The mood was one of focused urgency, with every team member aware that time was not on their side.

"Alright, let's prioritize our objectives based on the latest intelligence," Elise began, her voice steady, commanding attention. "We suspect The Order is planning something significant soon. We need to prevent this without tipping them off that we're closing in."

Leo, standing next to a large digital map highlighted with several locations, took the lead on detailing their approach. "Based on the recovered documents and the latest decrypts from their communications, we believe the 'Sanctuary of Stars' mentioned is likely located in the northern part of the city, near the old mining quarries."

Pointing to the map, he continued, "We've narrowed it down to three possible sites. Each location has historical significance, which fits the profile for their activities."

Elise nodded, assessing the map. "We'll need to set up surveillance at each site without being noticed. Use unmarked vehicles and plainclothes teams. I don't want them to have any indication we're onto them."

A tactical leader, Captain Jones, chimed in from the side of the table. "We've prepared three units for reconnaissance. They're ready to move out on your command. Each team has been briefed on maintaining cover and minimizing engagement unless absolutely necessary."

"Good," Elise replied, her gaze sharp. "Leo, coordinate with the tech team. Make sure all communication lines are secure. We can't afford any leaks. Have them monitor any unusual activity around these areas, especially at night."

Leo jotted down a note, then responded, "I'll ensure all teams have encrypted radios and that our tech specialists are on this 24/7. We'll use drones for additional aerial surveillance during off-peak hours to reduce the risk of being spotted."

Elise looked around the room, meeting the eyes of each team leader. "This is a critical phase. Our success not only depends on finding the sanctuary but also on understanding what The Order plans to do there. Any slip-up could escalate the situation."

Captain Jones asked, "Are we considering the possibility of needing to intervene during their ritual? If it comes to that, we need a plan for a safe and effective intervention."

"Yes, prepare an intervention strategy," Elise confirmed. "Non-lethal tactics as far as possible. We aim to disrupt and contain. I want a detailed plan on my desk by tomorrow morning."

As the meeting drew to a close, Leo added a final point. "Keep in mind, everyone, these are not typical criminals. They believe deeply in what they're doing. Expect resistance and, potentially, unpredictable behavior."

The team members nodded in understanding, each aware of the complex dynamics involved in confronting a group driven by fervent beliefs.

As the room cleared, Elise and Leo stayed behind, reviewing the maps and plans once more. "Think we're missing anything?" Elise asked, her tone indicating the weight of responsibility she felt.

Leo reviewed his notes, then shook his head. "I think we've covered all bases. Now, it's about execution and hoping we can catch them before they make their move."

Elise sighed, a rare moment of vulnerability showing through her composed exterior. "We'll stop them, Leo. We have to."

With a final look at the maps, they left the strategy room, ready to set their plans in motion. The race against time was not just about strategy and surveillance; it was a test of their ability to outthink and outmaneuver an adversary shrouded in mystery and driven by dangerous convictions.

Under the cloak of early evening, Elise Bennett and Leo Marquez coordinated the deployment of surveillance teams to the three suspected sites around the old mining quarries. With the locations spread out and terrain challenging, the operation required precise timing and stealth.

Elise checked in with the first team via her radio, her voice low and clear. "Team One, status report."

"Team One in position, no activity observed at the south quarry. Surveillance is set and operational," came the crisp response over the radio.

Leo was coordinating with the tech team, ensuring that all video feeds were streaming real-time data back to the mobile command center. "Make sure we have overlapping fields of view. I don't want any blind spots," he instructed the tech officer, who nodded and adjusted some controls.

As night fell, the teams settled into a tense vigil. The command center was abuzz with activity, with multiple screens showing different angles of the quarries. Elise walked between the stations, her eyes sharp as she monitored the feeds.

"Anything from Team Two?" she asked, stopping by the station that handled thermal imaging.

"Team Two reports all quiet at the northeast site. Thermal scans show no unusual heat signatures," reported the officer in charge of surveillance.

Leo, who had been discussing contingency plans, added his update. "Team Three at the western quarry has visual on two vehicles that arrived ten minutes ago. They're keeping a visual but staying out of sight."

"Keep me updated on any movement. If anyone approaches the ritual site, I want to know immediately," Elise directed, her focus returning to the main monitor.

The tension in the command center was palpable as hours passed with minimal activity. Each team member was acutely aware that the situation could change in an instant. The quiet of the night was periodically broken by soft updates and confirmations of status.

Around midnight, a sudden flurry of activity caught everyone's attention. "Movement at the western quarry," one of the surveillance officers announced, his voice urgent. "Multiple individuals congregating near the central area."

Elise and Leo approached the monitor, watching as the thermal imaging highlighted several figures moving together. "Looks like they're setting something up. Can we get audio?" Elise asked.

"Working on it now," the tech officer replied, adjusting some equipment to capture any sound from the area.

Leo's hand was steady on his radio, ready to coordinate a response. "Prepare Teams Two and Three for a possible intervention. Wait for my go."

As the audio came through, faint chants and the clattering of what sounded like ceremonial tools filled the command center. "They're starting something. We need to make a decision," Elise stated, her gaze fixed on the screen.

"We go on my mark. Non-lethal interventions only. We stop this ritual safely," Leo decided, his voice resolute. He gave the signal, and the teams moved in, their actions swift and coordinated.

From the command center, Elise and Leo watched as the operation unfolded. The feed showed the quick advance of their teams, the surprise on the faces of those gathered at the quarry, and the subsequent, orderly containment of the situation.

As the suspects were rounded up and the area secured, relief mixed with adrenaline pulsed through the command center. Elise took a deep breath, allowing herself a moment of satisfaction. "Good work, everyone. Let's start processing the scene. We need evidence of everything they were planning to do here."

Leo was already on his radio, coordinating the follow-up. "Secure all artifacts and documents. I want detailed photographs before anything is moved."

As the night progressed into the early hours of the morning, the successful interruption of the ritual marked a significant victory in their ongoing battle against The Order. Yet, as they debriefed back at the precinct, the weight of continuous vigilance remained ever-present, a necessary shield against the darkness they sought to keep at bay.

After the successful disruption of the ritual at the western quarry, Elise Bennett and Leo Marquez faced the task of interrogating the key participants captured during the raid. They hoped to glean information about any further plans or hidden elements of The Order that remained at large.

In a secure interrogation room, Elise sat across from one of the more elusive figures they had apprehended, known in The Order as Brother Samuel. Unlike previous detainees, Samuel had an air of calm defiance about him, his eyes steady and voice unwavering as he responded to Elise's questions.

"You understand why you're here, Samuel. Your group's activities have crossed legal boundaries. We need to know if there are other events planned," Elise stated, her tone firm yet open, inviting cooperation.

Samuel's response was measured. "Detective Bennett, I assure you, our goals are not meant to harm but to enlighten. However, I cannot provide details about activities I deem spiritual."

Elise leaned forward slightly, her approach direct but respectful. "Enlightenment that leads to loss of life is a crime, not a spiritual journey. We found a body, Samuel. We stopped what looked like another dangerous event tonight. This isn't about beliefs; it's about preventing harm."

Samuel nodded slowly, his demeanor suggesting a consideration of her words. "I understand your perspective. It's your duty to uphold the law. But understand this—our convictions are deeply held. The path of enlightenment carries risks."

Leo, who had been observing quietly, interjected subtly to shift the focus. "Risks should never include innocent people, Samuel. If there's something you can tell us that might prevent further harm, now is the time."

The room fell silent for a moment as Samuel weighed his options. Eventually, he spoke, his voice a blend of resignation and steadfastness.

"I can tell you this—there are no further 'events' planned, as you call them. Tonight was to be a significant moment, and it seems you have prevented it."

Elise and Leo exchanged a brief look, a mix of skepticism and relief palpable between them. "We'll need more than your word, Samuel. We need names, locations, anything that helps us ensure this is the end," Elise pressed, her voice steady.

Samuel shook his head slightly. "I have shared what I can. I must consider my brothers and sisters in faith."

As the interrogation wrapped up, with Samuel taken back to holding, Elise and Leo stepped into the dimly lit hallway outside, the weight of the night's events heavy upon them.

"That might be as much as we're going to get out of him," Leo remarked quietly, his voice tinged with frustration.

Elise nodded, her thoughts already racing ahead to the next steps. "It's something, at least. We'll cross-reference his statement with the evidence from the quarry. Maybe it will confirm his claim, or maybe it will open new leads."

As they walked back to the main office, their path lit only by the flickering lights overhead, the stillness of the precinct in the early hours felt like a brief respite in their ongoing battle. They knew the road ahead would be fraught with more challenges as they continued to unravel the complexities of The Order.

"This isn't over, is it?" Leo asked, a rhetorical question hanging between them.

"No, it's not," Elise responded, her voice resolute. "But tonight, we stopped them. Tomorrow, we'll keep pushing. We have to."

Their conversation faded as they reached the office, each preparing for the hours of work still ahead—work that would, they hoped, bring them closer to understanding and dismantling the shadowy network that had burrowed so deeply into the fabric of their city.

Chapter 11
The Fourth Victim

Elise Bennett and Leo Marquez were called to a grim scene on the outskirts of the city early in the morning. The chill of dawn had not yet lifted when they arrived at a secluded park, cordoned off by yellow tape with police officers milling around. The park, usually a place of tranquility, was now marred by the presence of a crime scene unit.

The body of a man lay near one of the walking paths, partially hidden by low-hanging branches of an old oak tree. His features were contorted in a grimace of fear, similar to the expression on the third victim, suggesting a horrifying realization before death.

As Elise and Leo approached, Detective Harris, who had arrived at the scene earlier, met them with a grim expression. "Looks like we're dealing with another ritual killing. It's got all the hallmarks of The Order."

Elise crouched beside the body, her experienced eyes quickly taking in the details. There were symbols carved into the tree above the body, and various objects that seemed to have been part of a ritualistic array were scattered around the scene.

Leo scanned the surroundings, his mind already ticking through the implications. "Any witnesses or anything from the nearby houses?"

"No," Harris replied, shaking his head. "It's been quiet, according to the locals. Whoever did this knew what they were doing and chose the time and place carefully."

The forensic team worked quietly around them, taking photographs and collecting evidence. Elise stood up, her gaze lingering on the sad tableau. "We need to ensure this doesn't escalate further. Each victim appears to have been more deliberately chosen, more methodically placed. This isn't random; it's a message."

Leo nodded, his jaw set firmly. "We'll increase patrols in the area and review all surveillance footage from nearby locations. I'll also have the team re-canvass the neighborhood, see if anyone saw anything odd around the time we estimate the victim was left here."

Elise looked back at the body, her mind racing with the urgency of their investigation. "We need to catch a break in this case soon. Someone out there knows what's happening, and we need to find them before anyone else gets hurt."

As they prepared to leave the scene, Leo placed a reassuring hand on Elise's shoulder. "We'll find them, Elise. We have to."

Their conversation was cut short by a call from the precinct. Another piece of evidence had been found at a different location, possibly related to the current string of ritualistic killings. With a brief nod to Harris to wrap up the scene, Elise and Leo hurried back to their vehicle, the weight of the case pressing down on them as the city slowly awoke around them.

As they drove away, the early morning sun broke through the trees, casting long shadows that seemed to echo the dark undercurrents of the case they were desperately trying to solve.

The sun had barely risen when Elise Bennett and Leo Marquez, along with a team of forensic experts, arrived at a second, remote location linked to the same string of mysterious occurrences. This time, they were deep in the woods, a place seldom visited by locals, known for its dense undergrowth and haunting silence.

As they approached the scene, the air grew noticeably cooler, the canopy of trees above blocking out the early morning light. A small clearing lay ahead, and it was here that the latest grim tableau had been set.

"Looks like we're too late again," Leo muttered as they stepped into the clearing. The scene was chilling—a circle of stones with various ritualistic symbols etched into them surrounded an area where the earth had been disturbed. In the center lay another body, positioned with arms outstretched and eyes open, staring blankly at the sky.

Elise knelt beside the body, her expression one of focused concern. "Same M.O. as the last one. Look at the arrangement of the stones and the symbols. It's almost a mirror image of what we saw at the park."

Detective Harris, who had followed them to the scene, glanced around nervously. "Do we think this is a continuation of the same pattern, then? Another message from The Order?"

"It seems so," Elise replied, standing up and taking a step back to view the entire scene. "Each killing more elaborate than the last. They're escalating, becoming bolder."

Leo crouched next to one of the stones, examining the symbols. "These aren't just random; they're specific, calculated. There's meaning here, something they're trying to communicate or achieve."

A forensic photographer moved through the scene, capturing every angle while another technician began collecting samples of the earth and the stones. Elise watched them work, her mind piecing together the fragments of the case.

"Every victim has been found in a place like this—remote, isolated," she said, mostly to herself. "It's as if the location is as important as the act."

"Yeah, it's like they're choosing these places for a reason," Leo added, standing up and dusting off his hands. "Maybe something to do with the natural elements? Or they're trying to avoid surveillance?"

Elise nodded. "Both, possibly. Let's make sure to map the locations of all the incidents. There could be a geographic pattern that we're missing."

Detective Harris, looking over the notes he had been taking, chimed in. "Should we be considering additional protection or surveillance at similar potential sites?"

"Definitely," Leo responded quickly. "I'll coordinate with the patrol units. Anything even remotely resembling these characteristics should be monitored closely."

As the sun climbed higher, filtering through the leaves and casting dappled shadows on the forest floor, the team continued their meticulous work. Elise stood at the edge of the clearing, her arms crossed, watching every move. The somber task of gathering evidence from the scene was a stark reminder of the urgency of their investigation.

"We'll need to go through all of this evidence with a fine-tooth comb," she stated firmly. "Let's get everything back to the lab for analysis as soon as possible. We might not have much time before the next incident."

Leo nodded in agreement, his face set in a grim line. "We'll crack this, Elise. We have to."

As they prepared to leave the scene, the reality of their situation weighed heavily on them. Each new discovery brought them closer to understanding the motivations behind these heinous acts, yet the identity and true intent of those responsible remained just out of reach.

Back at the precinct, the forensic lab was a flurry of activity as Elise Bennett and Leo Marquez oversaw the processing of the evidence collected from the two crime scenes. The meticulous task of analyzing each item was crucial in piecing together the motives and methods of The Order.

The lab, usually a place of clinical detachment, felt charged with a palpable sense of urgency. Technicians and forensic experts moved efficiently from one piece of evidence to another, documenting, photographing, and testing everything from ritualistic paraphernalia to soil samples taken from around the bodies.

Dr. Simmons, the lead forensic analyst, approached Elise and Leo with preliminary findings from the items gathered at the second crime scene in the woods. "We've identified some of the substances found on the stones arranged around the body. Several are common in ritualistic practices, but a few are quite rare and suggest a specific intention to induce altered states of consciousness."

Elise nodded thoughtfully. "That fits with the profile we're building. They're not just conducting rituals; they're creating experiences designed to impact deeply on participants."

Leo, reviewing photos of the symbols found at the scenes, added, "We need to understand the symbolism better. Could these be guiding the selection of victims or locations?"

"We're working on that," Dr. Simmons assured him, handing over a stack of enlarged photos. "Our consultant on occult practices has been giving us some insights, but it's complex. The symbols are esoteric, not standard by any means."

Meanwhile, a data analyst approached with a laptop, displaying a map of the city with the locations of all known incidents marked. "We've run a geographic analysis of the crime scenes and potential hotspots based on the ritualistic elements we've observed," she explained. "There's a pattern emerging that aligns with certain historical and astronomical significances."

"Good work," Elise responded, peering at the map. "Let's use this to predict potential future sites. We might be able to prevent another incident if we understand where they might strike next."

Leo, while discussing with another officer, received an update on the digital evidence recovery efforts. "The tech team has managed to recover deleted files from one of the laptops we seized. It looks like it contains communications between members of The Order discussing plans for future gatherings."

"That could be key," Elise said, turning to the tech team's supervisor. "I want a full report on those communications as soon as possible. Anything that helps us anticipate their next move."

As the team continued their analysis, Elise and Leo took a moment to step aside, gathering their thoughts. The pressure to stay ahead of The Order was immense, with each clue providing both hope and a reminder of the stakes involved.

"We're making progress," Elise stated, more to affirm to herself than to Leo. "Every piece of evidence gets us closer to understanding their plan and hopefully stopping them."

Leo looked over the bustling lab, his expression one of resolute determination. "We'll get them, Elise. We have the best team, and we're putting together the pieces faster than they can hide them."

As they prepared to continue their oversight of the evidence gathering, the partnership between Elise and Leo stood as a testament to their commitment to justice and safety. With each analyzed item and decoded message, they moved closer to disrupting the shadowy network that threatened their city, driven by the shared mission to protect and serve.

Late into the evening, Elise Bennett and Leo Marquez remained at the precinct, surrounded by files, forensic reports, and digital screens displaying ongoing analysis. The office was quiet except for the occasional murmur of discussion between team members as they pieced together the emerging picture of The Order's activities.

Elise, examining a series of photographs from the crime scenes, broke the silence with a sense of urgency. "Leo, look at this," she said, holding up a photo showing a close-up of one of the ritualistic symbols. "This symbol here—it's identical to one found in an old manuscript about celestial alignments and rituals. It's more specific than we thought."

Leo leaned over to look at the photo closely. "That could explain the choice of locations and times for these events. They're not just random or convenient—they're specifically chosen for their symbolic significance."

Elise nodded, placing the photograph on the table. "Exactly. And according to the manuscript, this symbol is associated with a ritual meant to invoke protection. But something is off; these rituals resulted in harm, not protection."

Their discussion was interrupted by a call from one of the tech team members. "Detective Bennett, Detective Marquez, you'll want to see this," he said, motioning them over to his workstation.

The detectives approached, watching as the tech pulled up an encrypted email chain that had been recovered from a hard drive seized during the raid. "We've managed to decrypt these emails. They're between several high-ranking members of The Order. It looks like they were planning another major event, possibly within the next few days."

Leo's expression turned grave. "Can we pinpoint the location or time?"

"We're still working on that," the tech replied, scrolling through the emails. "The details are coded, but we're close to cracking it."

As they delved deeper into the digital evidence, another officer approached, her face conveying bad news. "Elise, Leo, we have a problem," she announced, holding up a report. "One of our surveillance teams at the suspected locations has gone silent. We can't reach them, and their last check-in was over two hours ago."

Elise's focus shifted immediately. "Which location?"

"The old mill site, north of the city," the officer responded. "It was one of the potential targets for their next gathering."

Leo reacted swiftly, grabbing his radio. "Get a response team ready. We need to check on our people and secure that site."

Elise, meanwhile, turned back to the tech. "Keep working on those emails. Any information could be crucial."

As Leo coordinated with the response team, preparing them for a potential confrontation or rescue operation, Elise reviewed the latest findings from the emails, piecing together possible meanings from the coded messages.

The precinct buzzed with heightened activity as teams prepared to move out. Elise joined Leo, who was gearing up. "We need to handle this carefully," she cautioned. "If they've taken our team, it could be a trap."

Leo nodded, checking his equipment one last time. "I know. We'll be on high alert. Let's just hope we're not too late."

With the response team ready, Elise and Leo left the precinct, heading towards the old mill site. The drive was tense, each passing minute amplifying their concern for their missing colleagues and the uncertainty of what they might find.

As they approached the site, the eerie quiet of the abandoned mill was unsettling. The team moved in with precision, sweeping the area, their senses on high alert for any sign of their colleagues or members of The Order.

The breakthrough in understanding the ritual's symbolism had given them a critical edge, but the setback of potentially compromised team members weighed heavily on their minds, a stark reminder of the ever-present danger lurking beneath the surface of their investigation.

Chapter 12
The Puppeteer's Taunt

The situation at the old mill site had escalated quickly. Elise Bennett and Leo Marquez, along with their response team, had arrived to find their missing surveillance team safe but shaken, having been briefly detained by members of The Order who had fled before the police arrived. Amidst the chaos, a chilling discovery was made—a cell phone was left behind by The Order, its screen displaying a new message.

Elise held the device, playing the video message to Leo and the rest of the team gathered in the makeshift command center they had set up near the site. On the screen, a masked figure, voice distorted, issued a stark warning.

"You have meddled in affairs far beyond your understanding," the figure began, his tone calm but menacing. "Your actions have consequences, and you are not prepared for what is to come. Cease your interference, or be swept away by the tide of change we are ushering in."

Leo, his expression grim, turned to Elise as the video ended. "They're not just reacting to our moves. It sounds like they're stepping up their plans."

Elise nodded, her mind racing. "This isn't just a warning; it's a provocation. They want us to back off, which means we're getting close to something they can't afford for us to discover."

"I agree," Leo said, turning to address the team. "We need to increase our vigilance. Assume that they are monitoring our movements more closely than we thought. We should also consider this a potential threat to the safety of everyone involved in this investigation."

A senior detective, Jenkins, who had been reviewing maps of the area, joined the conversation. "Should we reconsider our approach? Maybe we need to be less predictable, change up our patrol routes, our check-in times?"

"That's a good start," Elise responded. "Let's implement random patrols and stagger our shifts. Also, encrypt all communications from this point on. We can't afford any leaks or interceptions."

"Should we reach out to any other agencies for support? FBI? Homeland Security?" suggested another officer, keen on broadening the scope of their resources.

"Not yet," Leo decided after a moment's thought. "Let's keep this contained as much as we can for now. We don't know how deep this goes, and until we do, too many players might complicate things."

Elise glanced back at the phone, considering their next move. "I want a full digital forensic sweep on this device. Find out where it came from, any traces of where the video was shot, anything that can tell us more about who we're dealing with."

As the team dispersed to carry out their new orders, Elise and Leo took a moment to regroup. "This is turning into more than just a series of crimes," Elise mused aloud. "It's becoming a battle of wills."

Leo looked out towards the mill, now secured but still ominous in the fading light. "And it's a battle we can't afford to lose. Not just for the sake of the case, but for the safety of the city."

The weight of their responsibility hung heavily in the air as they prepared to leave the site. The threat was no longer just a shadowy group performing illegal activities, but a direct challenge to their authority and safety. As they drove back to the precinct, the streets seemed darker, the night more oppressive. But the resolve that hardened within them was clear—they would not be intimidated or deterred.

Back at the precinct, Elise Bennett and Leo Marquez gathered with their team in the digital forensics lab, the air tense with anticipation. The cell phone with the ominous message was now in the hands of their top digital analyst, Sandra, who was meticulously working to extract any additional data from it.

"Any luck breaking down where this video might have been shot?" Elise asked, leaning over Sandra's shoulder as she navigated through layers of security on the device.

"We're still working on it," Sandra replied, her fingers flying over the keyboard. "The video doesn't have any visible metadata—it was scrubbed clean, which means they knew what they were doing. But I'm running it through some enhancement software to see if we can pick up any background noise or reflected images that might give us a clue."

Leo folded his arms, watching the screen intently. "What about the origin of the phone? Anything on where it was purchased or any previous owners?"

"It was bought cash at a retail store six months ago, no ties to a real name," Sandra explained, pulling up the purchase history on another screen. "It's been used sparingly, mostly for data, no calls or texts that would link it to an individual."

As they digested this information, Detective Harris, who had been reviewing the video again, chimed in. "I've been thinking about the wording of the taunt—it's theatrical, deliberate. This isn't just about scaring us off; it's about control, showing us they can reach out whenever they want."

Elise nodded thoughtfully. "You're right. It's psychological, a power play. They want us to feel watched, second-guessing our moves."

"The language used, the delivery—it's all very calculated," Leo added. "This group isn't just a bunch of amateurs; they're organized and they're strategic."

Sandra suddenly straightened, a hint of excitement in her voice. "Hold on, I've got something here. There's a reflection in the video, something I missed before. It looks like a specific type of light fixture, one that's fairly unique."

She enhanced the image, revealing the outline of an ornate chandelier. "This type of fixture is common in older buildings, possibly historic ones. We can cross-reference this with known properties owned or used by The Order."

"Great catch, Sandra," Elise praised, her brain ticking through the possibilities. "Let's get a list of all historical buildings they've shown interest in before. And cross-check with any recent acquisitions that haven't been investigated yet."

As the team mobilized to follow these new leads, Leo reflected on their progress. "Every piece of information is crucial. We're peeling back their layers of secrecy, and every layer gets us closer to shutting them down."

Elise, although focused on the task at hand, allowed herself a moment of cautious optimism. "We're getting closer, Leo. I can feel it. They made a mistake leaving that phone behind, and mistakes mean they're getting desperate."

The team worked late into the night, cross-referencing data, checking historical records, and analyzing every scrap of evidence that might lead them closer to understanding the taunt and, more importantly, preventing The Order's next move. With each discovery, the path forward became a little clearer, and their resolve to end the threat grew stronger.

In the quiet of Elise Bennett's office, she and Leo Marquez sat across from Marcus Eldridge, the captured leader of The Order, brought from his cell for a crucial dialogue. Despite his imprisonment, Marcus maintained a composed, almost serene demeanor as he faced the detectives.

Elise initiated the conversation with a direct approach, her voice calm but firm. "Marcus, we've uncovered more about your group's activities, including the recent threats. It's time to talk about your real intentions."

Marcus looked between Elise and Leo, a faint smile playing at the corners of his lips. "Detective Bennett, I've always been open about our intentions—to awaken humanity to greater truths. The methods may be misunderstood, but the purpose is pure."

Leo leaned forward, his tone slightly more confrontational. "There's nothing pure about causing harm or fear. Your taunts and your rituals have real-world consequences. People are getting hurt."

Marcus's eyes narrowed slightly, his response measured. "The path to enlightenment is fraught with challenges. Not all are ready to face them."

Elise interjected, her patience thinning. "We're not here to debate philosophy, Marcus. We know about the planned events, the so-called 'Sanctuary of Stars.' It ends now."

Marcus sighed, the facade of tranquility slipping momentarily. "You may halt these events, but you cannot stop the movement. There are others who will carry on."

Leo's voice grew stern. "That's not good enough. We need names, locations. Help us prevent any more harm."

Marcus looked down, his expression contemplative. After a long pause, he spoke softly. "There is little I can do to change your course, but I urge you to consider what you are fighting against. It is not evil, merely a different understanding of the world."

Elise's response was sharp. "Understanding doesn't require victims."

The conversation continued, with Marcus providing vague references to other members and locations, but nothing concrete enough to act upon immediately. It was clear he was still protecting the core of The Order.

As they concluded, Elise stood up, her gaze steady on Marcus. "This isn't over. We will continue to dismantle your operations, piece by piece."

Marcus stood slowly, maintaining his composure. "As is your duty, Detective. But consider this—the ideas we have planted cannot be eradicated by arrests or interrogations. Ideas are bulletproof."

After Marcus was led away, Elise and Leo remained in the office, the weight of the conversation lingering in the air.

"He's still playing games," Leo said finally, frustration evident in his voice.

Elise nodded, her mind racing with their next steps. "He is, but he's also scared. They didn't expect us to push this hard."

"We'll keep pushing," Leo affirmed, his determination clear. "We'll crack this, Elise. For the victims, for the city."

As they left the office to join the rest of their team, their resolve was stronger than ever. The confrontation with Marcus had not yielded all the answers they hoped for, but it reinforced their commitment to stopping The Order, driven by a deeper understanding of the stakes involved in their battle against the shadows.

As the investigation intensified, Elise Bennett and Leo Marquez sat late into the evening in the precinct's strategy room, surrounded by maps, photos, and digital displays, piecing together every bit of intelligence they had gathered. The room buzzed with the low murmur of two detectives discussing their next move.

Elise leaned over a map pinpointed with various locations associated with The Order. "We need to anticipate their next step. Marcus isn't giving anything away directly, but his hints about others taking over suggest that we might see a power shift or a new strategy emerging."

Leo, who had been reviewing notes from their interrogation, looked up thoughtfully. "I agree. He's too calm, almost like he's certain we won't be able to stop them in time. We need to disrupt their communications, make them react to us instead."

"Exactly," Elise responded, tapping a location on the map that had seen increased activity. "This area here has had several reports of unusual gatherings. It's isolated enough to avoid casual witnesses but accessible to members of The Order."

"Let's set up surveillance. If we can catch them in the act, we can gather undeniable evidence," Leo suggested, his tone indicating he was ready to move forward with immediate action.

Elise nodded, picking up her phone to coordinate with their field teams. "I'll get a team on it tonight. We'll monitor any traffic in and out of the area. Any unknown vehicles or known associates show up, I want eyes on them."

As they set their plan into motion, their focused preparation was suddenly interrupted by an alert from one of their tech specialists. "Detectives, you need to see this," he called out from his workstation across the room.

Elise and Leo approached quickly, watching as the technician pulled up security footage from a camera near another site known for its links to The Order. The video showed a small group of individuals unloading boxes from a van into a nondescript building.

"Got them," the technician said, enhancing the video to show clearer images of the faces. "Two of these individuals are on our watch list. Looks like they're setting up for something."

"Can we get audio?" Leo asked, squinting at the screen as he tried to identify anything in the boxes that could tell them more about what was being planned.

"Working on it. The mics didn't pick up much from this distance, but I'll clean up the audio and see what I can get," the technician replied, already busy with the task.

Elise turned to Leo, her decision firm. "Let's prepare a raid. If they're moving supplies like this, they might be gearing up sooner than we thought."

Leo nodded in agreement. "I'll organize the team. We'll need to move fast."

The night deepened as they put their plans into action, the precinct a hive of activity as everyone prepared for the operation. With each team member clear on their role, they were a unified force against the shadowy threat of The Order.

As Elise geared up, her mind was a mix of adrenaline and cold focus. "This ends now," she murmured to herself, a quiet vow in the silent hum of the strategy room.

Leo, checking his equipment one last time, glanced at Elise with a nod. "We've got this, partner. Let's bring them down."

Together, they left the precinct, the early hours of the morning holding a promise of confrontation and, hopefully, resolution. As they drove towards the site, the city around them was oblivious to the drama unfolding, a drama that could define the safety and security of its citizens.

Chapter 13
Dark Revelations

The aftermath of the raid was still unfolding when Elise Bennett and Leo Marquez found themselves facing another unexpected challenge: the media had caught wind of their investigation into The Order. News vans lined the street outside the precinct, and reporters with microphones and cameras were eagerly awaiting any officers willing to comment.

Inside the precinct, Elise and Leo, along with Captain Roberts, the public affairs officer, gathered in a small conference room to strategize their approach to handling the media frenzy.

"We need to control the narrative here," Captain Roberts advised, looking between Elise and Leo. "The last thing we need is panic or misinformation spreading through the city."

Elise nodded in agreement, her expression serious. "We should emphasize the success of the raid without giving away specifics about The Order's activities. We can't afford to tip them off about what we know."

Leo added, "It's also a chance to reassure the public. Let them know we're on top of this and their safety is our priority."

Captain Roberts prepared a brief statement for them to give to the press. "Keep it vague but positive. Acknowledge the ongoing investigation, but don't go into details about the arrests or the evidence we've collected."

As they stepped outside to face the reporters, the flash of cameras and the murmur of questions filled the air immediately.

Elise stepped up to the microphones first, her demeanor calm and authoritative. "Thank you for being here. I want to assure the public that last night's operation was a success. We conducted a raid that has helped us gather significant evidence in an ongoing investigation into a group that has posed a serious threat to our community."

A reporter from a major news outlet raised a hand, calling out, "Detective Bennett, can you tell us more about this group? Are they terrorists?"

Elise responded carefully, "We are investigating all aspects of this group's activities. It's part of a broader effort to ensure the safety of our citizens. I can't categorize them specifically at this time, but we are working closely with our federal partners to address any and all threats."

Leo then took a turn to add a reassuring tone. "Our teams performed exceptionally well, and there were no injuries during last night's operation. It's a testament to the professionalism and dedication of our officers who are committed to keeping this city safe."

Another reporter asked, "Is there an ongoing threat? Should people be worried?"

Leo answered, "While our investigation is ongoing, we believe we have mitigated any immediate threats through our recent actions. We always encourage the public to remain vigilant and report any suspicious activities to law enforcement."

As the press conference continued, Elise and Leo managed to navigate the barrage of questions with a mix of diplomacy and restraint, giving away no critical details while still providing a narrative that would satisfy the media's hunger for information.

After the reporters dispersed, Elise and Leo returned inside, both relieved.

"That went better than I expected," Leo remarked as they walked back to their office.

Elise gave a small smile, "Yes, but we'll need to keep a close eye on how the media spins this. The last thing we need is for The Order to know just how close we are."

Their conversation was a reminder of the delicate balance they had to maintain—not just in investigating The Order but in managing the public perception of their work. As they prepared for the next phase of their investigation, the media maneuver was a crucial victory in maintaining that balance.

Just as the dust seemed to settle from the media storm, a new crisis unfolded that reminded Elise Bennett and Leo Marquez of the cunning nature of their adversaries. The precinct received an anonymous tip leading them to an abandoned warehouse on the outskirts of the city, a place that had not been on their radar.

The late afternoon sun was waning as they arrived at the scene, the shadows long and foreboding against the dilapidated structure. The building sat isolated, surrounded by overgrown weeds, its windows boarded up, giving it a haunted look. The air was thick with tension as Elise and Leo, along with their tactical team, prepared to enter.

Inside, the warehouse was vast and dimly lit by shafts of light piercing through cracks in the walls. The air was stale, heavy with the scent of rust and old wood. As they moved cautiously through the space, the eerie quiet was suddenly shattered by the sound of a television playing loudly from a corner room.

Elise signaled her team to approach with caution. The TV was set up like a macabre centerpiece in a small, cleared area, surrounded by candles that cast flickering shadows on the walls. On the screen played a loop of news coverage of their recent press conference, but it was what lay in front of the television that brought them to a standstill.

Arranged meticulously on the floor were photographs—each a picture of a team member involved in the investigation, marked with red crosses over their faces. Beside each photograph lay detailed dossiers, personal information that sent a chill down Elise's spine. It was a clear message: they were all being watched.

Leo, his voice low and steady, broke the heavy silence. "They're pushing back. This was meant to intimidate, to show us they can reach us personally."

Elise, her mind racing with the implications, responded with resolve. "This changes the stakes. We're dealing with someone who not only anticipates our moves but is also steps ahead in this twisted game."

They carefully documented the scene, taking photographs and collecting the dossiers for further analysis. The realization that each move they made was potentially under surveillance was unsettling, but it also hardened their resolve to end this cycle of manipulation and threat.

As night began to fall, they left the warehouse, the images of their own faces marked with crosses burned into their memory. The ride back to the precinct was quiet, each officer lost in their thoughts, the weight of the situation bearing down on them.

Back at her office, Elise reviewed the dossiers with Leo, each page a violation of their lives, their safety hanging in a precarious balance. "We need to increase security for everyone involved. Home checks, monitoring of communications. No one goes anywhere alone," she instructed, her tone brooking no argument.

Leo nodded in agreement, his mind on his family, his team. "We'll set up a briefing first thing tomorrow. Everyone needs to be aware of the situation and the precautions they must take."

This latest maneuver by The Puppeteer was a stark reminder that their adversary was not just a shadow behind ritualistic crimes but a direct and personal threat to them and their loved ones. As they prepared for what might come next, Elise and Leo knew that the battle was not just about catching a criminal—it was about protecting their own from the dark reach of The Puppeteer.

Back at the precinct, Elise Bennett and Leo Marquez gathered their core team in the main conference room to review the findings and discuss the broader implications of the threats they had received. The room was filled with a tense energy as detectives and analysts sat around the large table, each with a folder of information in front of them.

Leo started the meeting, his voice serious. "The dossiers we found not only contained personal information but also details about our investigation—strategies, plans, even our schedules. This indicates a deep level of infiltration or surveillance capability by The Order."

Elise picked up the thread, her expression grave. "We need to consider the possibility of an inside leak. It's uncomfortable, but we can't ignore it. Each of us needs to review our interactions, secure our communications, and double-check our information sources."

A detective from the cyber unit spoke up, "We've been monitoring all communication channels for unusual activity. So far, nothing overt, but we're enhancing our encryption methods and implementing additional security measures on all our networks."

"Good," Elise responded. "What about connections to other cases? This level of organization and reach—could they be linked to other criminal activities we've been tracking?"

Leo flipped through a folder, pulling out several sheets of paper. "Here's something. There's a pattern of property acquisitions by entities connected to The Order. These properties often align with historical or symbolic significance, much like the sites of the rituals."

A junior detective added, "I cross-referenced the properties with past unsolved cases in those areas. Several align with unexplained disappearances or reports of suspicious activities dating back years."

Elise leaned forward, her focus sharpening. "This could be our angle—historical patterns that lead us to their current operations. Let's dig deeper into every one of those properties. Any connection, no matter how slight, could lead us to their next move."

The team nodded, scribbling notes and murmuring agreements as they began to see the links forming a clearer picture of a deeply entrenched network.

Leo continued, "We also need to look at financial flows. Whoever is funding this has deep pockets. We trace the money, we might just find the head of the snake."

One of the financial analysts spoke up, "I've started tracing back through shell companies and obscure transactions. It's a maze, but there are patterns. I need more time, but I think we can pinpoint a few key sources of funding."

"Keep at it," Elise encouraged, her gaze sweeping the room. "Everyone, this is a critical moment for us. We're closer than ever to understanding their network and preventing further harm. I know it's personal now, but that should only strengthen our resolve."

As the meeting drew to a close, the team was reinvigorated with a sense of purpose. The threat against them had made the stakes all the more real, but it had also pulled them together, each member committed to the task at hand.

Elise and Leo stayed behind as the room cleared, reviewing the maps and charts spread out before them. "We're on the right track," Elise said, more to herself than to Leo. "Now we just need to stay one step ahead."

Leo nodded, his expression determined. "We'll get them, Elise. We'll get them all."

With that, they gathered their notes and prepared for the long hours ahead. Each clue they uncovered, every connection they made, brought them closer to dismantling The Order and protecting their city from the shadow that had fallen over it.

Late into the evening, as the precinct quieted down and the rush of the day's events began to ebb, Elise Bennett found herself in her office, surrounded by piles of case files and the dim glow of her desk lamp. She pored over the information, seeking the connections that had eluded them so far. The tapping of her computer keyboard was a rhythmic counterpoint to the racing of her thoughts.

Leo Marquez knocked softly on her open door, stepping inside with a concerned look. "Elise, you're still here. You should get some rest."

Elise looked up, a tired smile on her face. "I could say the same for you, Leo. But I think I'm onto something here."

Leo walked in, leaning against the desk. "What did you find?"

"It's not what I found, it's what I remembered," Elise replied, pushing aside a stack of papers to make room for her laptop. "When I was a rookie, I worked a case—missing persons, no leads, no connections. It went cold, and it's haunted me. But now, thinking about The Order, their patterns... I dug up the old files. Look at this."

She turned the laptop toward Leo, showing him a map with several marked locations. "These disappearances happened near properties that The Order now owns. It can't be a coincidence."

Leo studied the screen, his brow furrowed. "That's a hell of a connection. But why didn't we see it before?"

"We weren't looking for it," Elise said, leaning back in her chair. "We didn't know what we were dealing with then. But now, we see their pattern—their signature."

The revelation brought a new perspective to their investigation, linking past mysteries with their current challenges. It underscored the depth and longevity of The Order's influence and made their task all the more daunting.

"Let's take this to the team first thing tomorrow," Leo suggested, his voice firm. "We'll re-open those cold cases, see if we can connect them directly to current members or activities of The Order."

Elise nodded, her mind already racing ahead. "And I'll contact the families. They deserve to know that we might finally have a lead."

The weight of the past and the urgency of the present melded into a renewed determination. They worked into the night, revisiting old evidence with new eyes, tracing the threads that had once seemed isolated but now appeared to be part of a larger, darker tapestry.

As dawn began to light the edges of the sky, Elise finally leaned back, allowing herself a moment to breathe. The night had been long, and the work grueling, but the pieces were coming together. They were closer than ever to understanding the scope of The Order's reach and to potentially stopping them.

Leo stood, stretching his stiff muscles. "I'll see you in a few hours. Get some rest, Elise. We're going to need all our strength for what's coming."

Elise nodded, her fatigue evident but her spirit undimmed. "Thanks, Leo. See you soon."

With a last look at the screen, she finally shut her laptop, her thoughts still swirling with the possibilities of what they had uncovered. The personal revelation had not only rekindled her resolve but had also reminded her why she had become a detective: to fight the shadows and bring light to those who had been lost in the darkness.

As she left the precinct, the first rays of the morning sun painted the sky with hues of gold and pink, a daily rebirth that mirrored her renewed hope to bring closure to the families haunted by loss. The city was waking up, and so was the case that could change everything.

Chapter 14
Underground Secrets

Elise Bennett and Leo Marquez stood at the entrance of an abandoned subway station, its rusted sign barely clinging to the archway. The air was thick with the musty smell of dampness and decay. Their flashlights cut through the darkness, revealing graffiti-covered walls and debris strewn across the floor. This forgotten part of the city had been identified as a potential meeting place for The Order, based on the patterns and clues uncovered from the last raid.

"This place gives me the creeps," Leo murmured, his light sweeping over a faded mural.

"It's not meant to be welcoming," Elise replied, checking her watch. "According to the files, they used locations like this for initiations. Isolated, secretive, perfect for their needs."

They proceeded down the crumbling steps, each step echoing in the vast emptiness. As they reached the platform, the beam from Elise's flashlight fell on a series of symbols spray-painted along the wall—symbols that matched those found in the dossiers from The Order.

"Looks like we're in the right place," Leo noted, taking pictures of the symbols with his camera. "These match the initiation rites described in Marcus's journals."

Elise nodded, her eyes scanning the dark corners of the station. "Let's spread out. Look for any evidence that they've been here recently."

As they separated, their radios kept them connected, a lifeline in the oppressive gloom. Elise moved towards an old ticket booth, its glass broken, the inside filled with old newspapers and rat nests. She used her gloved hand to sift through the debris, looking for anything that didn't belong.

"Elise, you find anything?" Leo's voice crackled through the radio.

"Just trash so far," she responded, pulling out a water-damaged book with indiscernible cover art. "Nothing significant yet."

Meanwhile, Leo explored the far end of the platform, where he discovered a hidden door partially concealed by shadows and debris. "Elise, come over here. Found something."

Joining him, Elise shone her light on the door. It was steel, heavier than typical subway architecture. "This wasn't part of the original station design. It's been added."

Using their combined strength, they managed to pry the door open, the metal groaning as it gave way. Beyond lay a narrow tunnel, the walls rough and seemingly hand-carved, extending deeper into the darkness.

"This doesn't look official," Leo said, peering into the abyss. "No telling how far it goes or what we'll find."

Elise pulled a compact digital camera from her belt. "Let's document everything. We might need to show this to the city engineers. Could be part of a larger network."

As they ventured into the tunnel, the air grew cooler and more stagnant. They found themselves walking down a gentle incline, the floor slippery with moisture. Every now and then, they would stop to mark their path, ensuring they could find their way back.

After about a hundred meters, the tunnel opened into a larger chamber. It was eerily silent, save for the distant drip of water. Their lights revealed several objects: candles, a few old books, and what looked like a makeshift altar.

"It's definitely been used by The Order," Elise concluded, examining a book that contained names and dates. "These look like records of meetings or ceremonies."

Leo, who had been inspecting the altar, held up a small, metallic object. "Found this. Looks like one of the ceremonial tokens we read about in the seized documents."

"We'll need to collect all of this," Elise decided, her voice echoing slightly in the chamber. "Every piece could help us understand their operations better."

They spent the next hour photographing and collecting evidence, speaking little as they focused on their tasks. When they finished, they made their way back to the surface, the weight of their discovery pressing down on them.

Emerging from the station, Elise took a deep breath of the fresh air. "This is bigger than we thought, Leo. That tunnel could be one of many."

Leo nodded, his face set in grim determination. "Let's get this evidence back. We'll need to plan our next move carefully."

As they drove back to the precinct, the city lights blurred past, a stark contrast to the darkness they had left behind. They were delving deeper not only into the physical underground but also into the dark heart of The Order.

Continuing their exploration of the underground network, Elise Bennett and Leo Marquez ventured deeper into a series of interconnected tunnels. The air was cool and musty, and their flashlight beams danced over ancient brickwork and newer concrete patches. The oppressive silence was broken only by the sound of their careful steps and the occasional drip of water from the ceiling.

As they moved, they encountered another steel door, this one sturdier and more foreboding than the last. Leo examined the lock, a modern electronic keypad nestled in the old frame.

"Looks like this door was meant to keep people out, or something in," Leo observed, his voice echoing slightly in the narrow space.

Elise pulled out her lock pick set, a tool she'd become proficient with over her years on the force. "Let's see if they updated their security protocols as much as their door hardware."

After a few tense minutes, the lock clicked open, and they slowly pushed the door forward. It creaked loudly, disturbing the quiet of the tunnel.

Beyond the door lay a large chamber, its walls lined with shelves filled with books, candles, and strange artifacts. In the center of the room stood a large table, covered with maps and various documents. The entire setup was illuminated by a series of small, battery-operated lamps.

Elise stepped inside first, her flashlight sweeping across the room. "This looks like a planning room or some kind of command center for The Order."

Leo followed, his attention drawn to the maps. "These are detailed layouts of the city—look, here are the locations we've been investigating. They've marked specific points of interest."

As they examined the documents, they realized the scope of The Order's planning. There were schedules, names, even contingency plans laid out with meticulous detail.

"This is a gold mine," Elise murmured, photographing the documents. "It looks like they were planning multiple operations. We've got to get this back to the team."

Leo picked up a small, leather-bound book from the table. Opening it, he found it filled with names and notes in a tight, careful script. "Seems like a ledger or a membership list. This could help us finally put names to faces and roles within The Order."

They continued to search the chamber, collecting evidence and documenting everything. As they worked, Elise's radio crackled to life. It was Captain Roberts, checking in from the precinct.

"Elise, Leo, what's your status?"

"We've found a major hub," Elise responded, her voice a mix of excitement and gravity. "Gathering evidence now. This place is a treasure trove of information."

"Understood," came the reply. "Be cautious, we don't know if you're alone down there."

Acknowledging the warning, Elise glanced at Leo, a silent agreement passing between them to hasten their efforts.

As they prepared to leave, Leo noticed a small, almost hidden drawer in the table. Pulling it open, he found a series of photographs. "Elise, come see this."

She joined him, looking down at the photos, which showed different members of The Order at various events. Some of the faces were familiar from their investigations. But one photo caught her eye—it was a recent picture of Marcus, apparently leading a ceremony.

"They were still taking orders from him," Leo noted, studying the picture. "Even possibly planning a breakout or some way to get him back."

"We need to alert the security at the detention center," Elise said quickly, already reaching for her radio. "And let's wrap up here. We have enough to start putting some serious pressure on The Order."

With the evidence they needed bagged and tagged, they made their way back through the tunnels, the weight of their discovery pressing upon them. They had uncovered more than just plans; they had found the heart of The Order's underground activities. As they emerged into the night, the reality of their discovery settled in, ready to be unraveled back at the precinct.

Back at the precinct, Elise Bennett and Leo Marquez sat with a team of experts in a small, cluttered conference room. The table was strewn with the various artifacts, books, and documents recovered from the hidden chamber, each item potentially a key to unlocking the secrets of The Order.

Dr. Harold Finch, a consultant specializing in esoteric religions and cryptic languages, was examining one of the more ornate books they had found. His fingers traced the symbols on the page, his brow furrowed in concentration.

"Any luck, Harold?" Elise asked, watching him closely.

Dr. Finch looked up, excitement evident in his eyes. "Yes, I think I've made a significant breakthrough. This text is not just ritualistic—it's a manual of sorts. It outlines specific ceremonies meant to harness what they believe are powerful cosmic energies."

Leo leaned in, intrigued. "Can you tell what the purpose of these ceremonies might be?"

Dr. Finch flipped the book around to show them a detailed diagram. "See here? This ceremony was set for the next full moon, which is just three days from now. According to this, it's not merely a gathering—it's an initiation rite designed to amplify the group's power."

Elise processed this information, her mind racing. "An initiation rite— could this be what they planned to use to expand their influence?"

"Possibly," Dr. Finch replied, nodding. "And there's more. It mentions a location not previously known to us—a secluded estate outside the city.

If my translation is correct, this is likely where they intend to hold the ceremony."

Leo picked up his phone, ready to act. "I'll get a team to scout the location. If we move fast, we might catch them setting up."

Elise turned to Dr. Finch, "Harold, is there anything in that text about how to disrupt these rites? If we can't stop them from gathering, maybe we can interfere with the ceremony itself."

Dr. Finch considered for a moment before responding. "There are mentions of specific artifacts essential to their rituals. Without them, the ceremony might not only be disrupted but could backfire according to their beliefs."

"That's good to know," Elise said thoughtfully. "Leo, make sure the team looks for any unusual artifacts. Anything that doesn't belong in a normal house setting could be what we're looking for."

As plans were put into motion, Elise continued to discuss the findings with Dr. Finch, probing deeper into the nature of The Order's beliefs and tactics. "Harold, how deeply are these beliefs ingrained? Could exposing or discrediting them publicly sway the group's followers?"

"It's possible," Dr. Finch answered, closing the book with care. "Groups like this often rely on secrecy and the mystique of hidden knowledge. Pull back the curtain, and you may well diminish their power."

"Then let's prepare to pull back that curtain," Leo declared, standing up. "I'll coordinate with the public affairs office. Once we disrupt this ceremony, we'll make sure everyone knows how dangerous and deluded this group is."

With each member of the team clear on their role, they set about their tasks with renewed vigor. Elise stayed behind with Dr. Finch, going over more texts, searching for any detail that might have been overlooked.

As the meeting broke up, the gravity of their upcoming confrontation with The Order weighed heavily on Elise. She knew that the next few days could be critical in ending the group's influence once and for all.

"Thank you, Harold," she said as Dr. Finch packed up his notes. "You may have just given us the edge we need."

Dr. Finch smiled, his demeanor calm. "Glad to be of service, Detective. Let's hope our efforts bring this to a safe conclusion."

Elise nodded, her resolve firm. "We'll make sure of it." As she left the room, her steps were purposeful; the battle lines were drawn, and she was ready to lead her team into what she hoped would be the final act in their long struggle against The Order.

As the team prepared to raid the estate mentioned in the discovered texts, Elise Bennett and Leo Marquez decided to conduct a preliminary reconnaissance of the location themselves. The estate, a sprawling old manor surrounded by dense woods, was as isolated as it was imposing.

Driving down the winding road that led to the estate, Leo glanced at Elise, who was reviewing the map and notes on her tablet. "We need a full picture of what we're dealing with before we bring in the team. Any last-minute surprises could jeopardize the whole operation."

Elise nodded, her eyes not leaving the screen. "Agreed. Let's keep a low profile. We need to confirm this is the right place without alerting anyone inside."

They parked their unmarked car a safe distance from the main gate and proceeded on foot, using the cover of the trees to approach the estate unseen. The manor loomed ahead, its windows dark, giving it a vacant, almost spectral appearance.

As they neared the back of the estate, Elise motioned for Leo to stop. She pointed to a figure moving stealthily among the shadows near the garden. "Look, someone's there."

They watched as the figure, a young woman, seemed to be carefully tending to some hidden objects in the underbrush. After a moment, she straightened up and turned to head back towards the house, giving Elise and Leo a clear view of her face.

Elise's breath hitched slightly. "That's Julia Mason. She was reported missing two years ago — thought to be one of The Order's recruits."

Leo, recognizing the urgency, whispered, "Let's follow her. She might lead us to something."

They kept their distance, trailing Julia to a small, secluded outbuilding behind the main house. Inside, they could hear voices, one of which was unmistakably giving instructions. The tone was authoritative, almost commanding.

Elise and Leo exchanged a look, and on silent agreement, they approached closer, positioning themselves near a window to listen.

"We must be ready by midnight. The alignment won't wait for us," said a male voice from inside. "Ensure everything is prepared according to the instructions. We cannot afford mistakes, not tonight."

Julia's voice responded, hesitant but clear. "Yes, I understand. But are you sure it's safe? After what happened last time…"

The man cut her off. "Safety is not our priority, Julia. Transformation is. You know this. You chose this path."

Unable to listen further without risking detection, Elise pulled Leo back. "We have enough. Let's call it in."

They moved quickly back to their car, Elise contacting their backup team. "We have confirmation. The estate is active, and they're planning something big for tonight. We move in at 2300 hours. Full breach and clear."

Leo drove them away from the estate, the weight of their discovery settling in. "You think Julia's part of this willingly?" he asked, a note of concern in his voice.

Elise shook her head, unsure. "I don't know. It sounded like she might be having doubts. We need to make sure she's safe when we go in."

As they returned to the precinct to prepare, the pieces of The Order's plan were becoming clearer, and so were the stakes. They were not just confronting a group of ritualistic fanatics; they were battling for the souls and safety of people like Julia, caught up in something far beyond their control.

That night, as they geared up, Elise felt the gravity of their task. They were not only law enforcers; they were rescuers in the truest sense. As the team assembled, her resolve hardened. Tonight would end with The Order dismantled, and its captives safe.

Chapter 15
Journalist's Clue

In the aftermath of the raid at the estate, Elise Bennett and Leo Marquez regrouped with their team at the precinct. The operation had been successful in many ways, yielding crucial evidence and disrupting The Order's planned ritual. However, the encounter had also raised new questions about the depth and reach of the organization's network.

The precinct's briefing room buzzed with a low hum of activity as officers and analysts worked to catalog and analyze the evidence collected from the estate. Amidst the organized chaos, Elise and Leo sat with their immediate team to reassess their strategy.

"We did good work last night," Elise began, her tone firm yet thoughtful. "We stopped them, for now. But it's clear from what we found that this goes deeper than we thought."

Leo, looking over the maps and documents laid out on the table, nodded in agreement. "The network is extensive. The connections we uncovered between The Order and historical sites around the city suggest they've been planning this for a long time."

As they discussed their next steps, Detective Harris interjected with a crucial update. "We've finished processing the digital devices recovered from the estate. Found something interesting—a series of communications between Marcus and an unknown contact. It seems they were cautious, but one message stood out. It mentioned a 'key piece' that would ensure the success of their operations."

Elise leaned forward, her interest piqued. "Any idea what this 'key piece' refers to?"

"No," Harris replied, shaking his head. "It's vague, could be anything from an artifact to information. But it's definitely something they value highly."

The conversation was momentarily interrupted as an officer approached the group, handing Elise a note. "Detective Bennett, you have a call. Line two. It's urgent."

Excusing herself, Elise walked over to the phone, her mind racing with possibilities. She picked up the receiver, her voice calm. "This is Bennett."

The voice on the other end was brisk, slightly anxious. "Detective Bennett, this is Tim Norton. I'm a journalist with the City Times. I've been following your case on The Order, and I think I have something that might interest you."

Elise was initially skeptical, aware of the media's eagerness to sensationalize. "What kind of information are we talking about?"

"I've been researching The Order for months," Tim explained. "Came across an old journal at a private auction—turns out it belonged to one of the founding members. It's filled with references to a plan, something they've been working towards for decades. I believe it's connected to what you're investigating."

Elise's skepticism gave way to curiosity. "Can we meet? I'd like to see this journal."

"Absolutely," Tim replied. "I'm at my office downtown. When can you come by?"

"As soon as I can. I'll be there within the hour," Elise said, her tone decisive.

Hanging up the phone, she returned to the group, her expression serious. "That was a journalist who claims to have a journal connected to The Order. I'm going to check it out. Leo, can you handle things here?"

Leo nodded, his gaze following Elise as she gathered her things. "Of course. Keep your phone on, and be careful."

As Elise left the precinct, the weight of their ongoing investigation pressed upon her. The journal could be a significant breakthrough, shedding light on The Order's long-term objectives and perhaps revealing the identity of the mysterious 'key piece' they needed to fully dismantle the group's plans.

Elise Bennett arrived at the *City Times* office, a nondescript building nestled between a café and a bookstore in a busy part of downtown. The reception was quiet, save for the soft click of keyboards and the occasional ring of a phone. She approached the reception desk, badge in hand.

"I'm here to see Tim Norton," Elise announced to the receptionist, a young woman with sharp eyes and a tidy bun.

"Just a moment, Detective Bennett," the receptionist replied, pressing a button on her phone. "Mr. Norton, Detective Bennett is here to see you."

"Send her up, please," came a voice from the intercom.

The receptionist gestured toward the elevator. "Fifth floor, ma'am. Last door on your right."

As Elise reached the fifth floor and approached Tim Norton's office, the door swung open before she could knock. Tim stood in the doorway, a man in his mid-thirties with a keen gaze and a stack of papers in one hand.

"Detective Bennett, thank you for coming on such short notice," Tim greeted her, stepping aside to let her into his office, which was cluttered with books, newspapers, and multiple computer screens.

"Thank you for contacting me," Elise said, taking a seat across from his desk. "You mentioned a journal connected to The Order?"

"Yes, right here," Tim said, placing an old, leather-bound book on the desk between them. "I found it last month at an estate sale. It belonged to a man named Harold Greaves, identified in several of my other sources as one of the early members of The Order."

Elise opened the journal, her eyes scanning the handwritten pages. "This could be incredibly valuable. What exactly did you find in here that relates to our case?"

Tim leaned forward, his enthusiasm evident. "There are several mentions of a long-term plan called 'The Ascension.' It's sort of cryptic, but it seems to involve significant historical and astrological events. From what I can gather, it might culminate soon."

"That aligns with some of what we've discovered," Elise noted, her mind racing. "Did Greaves mention anything about a 'key piece'?"

"Yes, actually," Tim replied, flipping through the journal to a marked page. "Here it says, 'The key will unlock the final gate when the stars align.' It's mentioned alongside a ritual date that's just a few weeks from now."

Elise's pulse quickened. "This could be what we've been looking for. Can I take this to our forensics team to verify its authenticity and examine it more closely?"

"Of course," Tim said, but as he spoke, his office phone rang. He paused to answer it, his brow furrowing as he listened. "Yes, this is Norton... What? When?"

Elise watched as his expression changed from curiosity to concern. He hung up the phone abruptly.

"I need to go," Tim said quickly. "There's been a break-in at my apartment. They might have been looking for this journal."

"I'll come with you," Elise offered immediately. "Whoever did this could be connected to The Order. They might still be there."

As they hurried out of the office and down to the street, Elise contacted Leo to update him on the situation and request backup at Tim's apartment.

The ride to Tim's apartment was tense, each traffic light a frustrating delay. Elise's mind was on the journal and its implications. The potential connection between the journal and the break-in was too significant to ignore, and she knew that they had to act quickly to protect any evidence that might remain.

Arriving at the apartment, they found the door ajar, the lock obviously tampered with. Elise drew her weapon, motioning for Tim to stay back as she carefully entered the apartment, ready for an unexpected encounter that might reveal even more about the shadowy figures pulling the strings of The Order.

After ensuring Tim Norton's apartment was secure and that no further threats were present, Elise Bennett discussed their next steps. The apartment had been ransacked, presumably by someone looking for the journal or anything related to it. Fortunately, Tim had taken the journal with him to the office, unknowingly thwarting the intruder's search.

Back in Tim's cleared living room, amidst the disarray of papers and personal items, Elise and Tim sat down to discuss how to leverage the media to their advantage, now realizing the potential risks and rewards involved.

"Tim, this attempt on your apartment shows that we're up against someone who's not just watching, but actively trying to interfere," Elise began, her tone serious but reassuring. "We can use this to our advantage. We need to control the narrative and use the media to expose The Order before they regroup."

Tim, still visibly shaken but resolute, nodded in agreement. "I agree. The public needs to know what's going on. The City Times can run a story on this. We can expose The Order's activities and how deep this goes. It could help bring forth witnesses or others who've been too scared to come forward."

"Exactly," Elise replied. "We also need to highlight the risks to those connected to the case. It might provide us with more protection and more eyes on the lookout for any suspicious activities."

Tim leaned forward, his journalist instincts kicking in. "I can start drafting an article tonight. I'll need some details from you—nothing that jeopardizes the investigation, of course, but enough to make the threat clear and present."

Elise considered this for a moment. "You can outline the historical context of The Order, mention the recent raids, and the fact that evidence points to a larger, more imminent threat. Emphasize that law enforcement is on high alert and that public safety is our top priority."

"Should we mention the journal directly?" Tim asked, tapping his pen against his notebook.

"Only in broad terms," Elise decided. "Mention that new evidence has come to light which could be pivotal in understanding the scope of The Order's plans. But leave out specifics that could make the journal a target again."

Tim scribbled notes as they spoke, his professional demeanor regaining its edge despite the earlier chaos. "I'll need a quote from you, something strong and reassuring, to close out the article."

Elise thought for a moment, then said, "You can say, 'The police are dedicated to ensuring the safety of the city and its residents. We are uncovering significant leads that will help us put an end to any threat posed by this group. We encourage anyone with information to come forward. Your city needs you.'"

"That's solid," Tim said, nodding as he wrote. "I'll have a draft ready within the hour. We can go to print by morning."

As they wrapped up their discussion, Elise's phone buzzed—a message from Leo, asking for an update. She quickly texted him back, informing him of their plan to use the media as a strategic tool in the investigation.

"This is a good move, Tim," Elise said, standing to leave. "Thank you for being brave enough to stand with us on this."

Tim stood as well, extending his hand. "Thank you, Detective. Let's bring them down together."

Elise left Tim's apartment, feeling a mix of apprehension and hope. Leveraging the media was a gamble, but given the stakes, it was one they needed to take. As she drove back to the precinct, the city lights blurred past, each one a reminder of the lives they were working to protect.

In the quiet solitude of her office, Elise Bennett pored over the historical data and evidence that Tim Norton's journal had brought to light. She was deep in thought, connecting the dots from past cases to the current activities of The Order, when Leo Marquez knocked and entered, holding a folder filled with old case files.

"Elise, you might want to take a look at this," Leo said as he approached her desk, laying the folder down. "I've been going through cold cases from the areas surrounding the properties owned by The Order. Found something that might interest you."

Elise looked up, her focus shifting as she opened the folder. It contained a detailed report on a series of unexplained disappearances dating back nearly two decades—cases that had gone cold without any leads.

"These disappearances happened in a pattern, almost cyclically, every few years. They all occurred near the locations we now know were being used by The Order for their gatherings," Leo explained.

Elise scanned the documents, her mind racing. "This could be the link we've been missing. If we map out these disappearances with the timeline of The Order's known activities, we might be able to predict their next moves or at least understand their operational cycle better."

Leo nodded, his expression serious. "There's more—look at this," he said, pointing to a faded photograph in the file. It showed a group of people at a community event, and in the background, partially obscured but unmistakable, was a younger Marcus Eldridge, the leader of The Order they had recently apprehended.

"This photo was taken a year before the first disappearance noted here," Leo continued. "Marcus was active in these communities long before he became a prominent figure in The Order."

Elise leaned back in her chair, absorbing the implications. "So he's been influencing these areas for decades, grooming them for his agenda. It's deeper than we thought."

"We need to bring this to the task force meeting tomorrow. It could help us tighten the net around current members and perhaps prevent future incidents," Leo suggested.

Elise agreed, her resolve hardening. "Let's do that. I'll compile a report tonight. We'll need every piece of evidence to build a strong case for a pattern of criminal activity under the guise of their rituals."

As Leo left her office, Elise turned her attention back to the files. She worked through the night, cross-referencing dates, locations, and events, creating a comprehensive timeline that detailed The Order's hidden influence over the years. Each piece of data added weight to their theory and brought them closer to understanding the true scope of The Order's reach.

By morning, Elise had a detailed presentation ready. She arrived at the task force meeting with a sense of purpose, ready to share her findings with the team. As she laid out the timeline, showing the correlation between the cold cases and The Order's activities, the room was filled with a focused intensity. Her presentation provided not only a historical perspective but also a crucial lead that could guide their ongoing efforts.

With this new information, the task force was better equipped to anticipate The Order's movements and prepare for the challenges ahead. Elise's work had not only connected past atrocities to present dangers but also paved the way for preventative measures that could save lives in the future. As the meeting concluded, there was a renewed sense of urgency and a collective commitment to bringing The Order to justice, once and for all.

Chapter 16
Chasing Shadows

Elise Bennett and Leo Marquez sat in their unmarked police car, staking out the suburban home of Dr. Helena Shaw, a psychologist whose name had surfaced repeatedly in their investigation. According to their information, Dr. Shaw had been providing counseling services to several members of The Order, and they believed she might hold key insights into the group's psychological manipulation tactics.

Leo checked his watch and then glanced at Elise. "Do you think she's even aware of what her clients are involved in?"

"It's hard to say," Elise replied, adjusting her rearview mirror to keep a better eye on the front door of the beige, two-story house. "She could be a knowing participant, or she might just be an unwitting tool in their operations. Either way, we need to find out what she knows."

The front door of the house opened, and Dr. Shaw appeared. She was a middle-aged woman with sharp features and a brisk manner. Locking the door behind her, she descended the front steps and headed towards a silver sedan parked in the driveway.

"Now's our chance," Elise said. They exited their car and approached Dr. Shaw just as she was about to get into her vehicle.

"Dr. Shaw?" Elise called out.

Dr. Shaw turned, a look of mild surprise crossing her face. "Yes? Can I help you?"

"I'm Detective Elise Bennett, and this is my partner, Detective Leo Marquez. We're with the city police department," Elise explained, showing her badge. "We'd like to ask you a few questions about your professional interactions with certain individuals."

Dr. Shaw regarded them both warily. "Is there something wrong? Have any of my clients done something illegal?"

"We're more concerned about who your clients might be involved with," Leo interjected smoothly. "Specifically, their connections to a group known as The Order."

Dr. Shaw's expression tightened slightly. "I'm bound by confidentiality not to discuss my clients or their situations. Unless you have a warrant, I'm afraid I can't help you."

"We understand your position, Dr. Shaw, and we respect the confidentiality you maintain," Elise said earnestly. "However, this is a matter of public safety. Your cooperation could potentially prevent serious crimes."

Dr. Shaw paused, considering their words. "I still can't give you names or details. But I can say that I've noticed a troubling pattern among some of my clients. They exhibit a dependency not typical of my usual cases. It's almost cult-like."

"That's consistent with what we know about The Order," Leo noted. "They manipulate their members' emotional and psychological states. Anything more you can share might be crucial."

Dr. Shaw sighed, a conflicted look crossing her face. "I can tell you that many of these clients were referred to me by the same person, though I never met them directly. All communications were done via email."

"Do you still have access to those emails?" Elise asked, her tone hopeful.

"Yes, they should be in my office records. I can forward them to you, but I'll need to ensure that doing so is within legal bounds," Dr. Shaw responded, her professionalism evident.

"We appreciate any assistance you can provide," Elise said, handing Dr. Shaw her card. "Please send anything you find to this secure email address.

And, if you think of anything else, no matter how insignificant it might seem, don't hesitate to contact us."

Dr. Shaw nodded, taking the card. "I'll do what I can. I must protect my clients, but I also don't want to enable criminal activity."

"Thank you, Dr. Shaw. You're helping more than you know," Leo added as they concluded their conversation.

As they returned to their car, Elise felt a mix of frustration and hope. "Let's hope she comes through with those emails. It could be the lead we've been waiting for."

Leo started the car, pulling away from the curb. "Every piece helps, Elise. We're getting closer."

Their conversation faded as they drove back to the precinct, each lost in their thoughts, contemplating the complex web of psychological control at the heart of The Order and hoping that Dr. Shaw's cooperation would shine a light into those dark corners.

Back at the precinct, Elise Bennett and Leo Marquez convened in the digital forensics lab, surrounded by monitors displaying lines of code and encrypted communications. They were waiting for the digital forensics team to trace the origins of the emails Dr. Shaw promised to send, which could potentially lead them to more members of The Order.

As they watched, a technician, named Erica, flagged them down. "Detectives, we've got something coming through from Dr. Shaw's office. I'm tracing the source of the emails now."

"Good work, Erica. Let us know the moment you find anything that can point us in the right direction," Elise said, leaning closer to view the screen.

Leo added, "Any anomalies or patterns in those emails could be key. Keep an eye out for repeated phrases or any references to locations or events."

Erica nodded, her fingers flying over the keyboard as she worked. "Here's something interesting. The emails came from several encrypted sources, but they all funnel through the same server. It's a private server, looks like it's based out of a remote location north of the city."

"That could be their main hub, or at least a significant relay point for their operations," Elise mused. "Can we pinpoint the exact location?"

"Working on that now," Erica replied. Her screen flickered as maps and data grids popped up. "Got it. It's a small compound, fairly isolated, owned by a shell company that links back to a known associate of Marcus Eldridge."

Leo's eyes narrowed. "That's our next target then. We need to prepare a raid."

"Wait," Elise interjected, her gaze still fixed on the screen displaying the flow of email communications. "Let's not rush in. This server might be our only lead to higher-ups in The Order. If we tip them off, we might lose them for good."

Leo considered this, then nodded in agreement. "You're right. Let's keep monitoring the server. See if we can intercept more communications. Maybe we can gather enough intel to take down more than just one compound."

Elise turned to Erica, "Keep this server under constant surveillance. Alert us to any unusual activity or any attempts to take it offline."

"Will do," Erica confirmed, already adjusting her monitoring setup to provide real-time alerts.

As they stepped out of the lab, Elise and Leo discussed their broader strategy. "Once we gather enough evidence, we'll coordinate with the FBI. This is bigger than just our jurisdiction," Elise stated.

Leo agreed, "I'll reach out to our federal contacts. Let them know what we're onto and see how they can assist. The wider we cast our net, the more we can catch."

Their conversation was interrupted by a call from Captain Roberts, their superior. "Bennett, Marquez, in my office, now. We've got a situation developing with our media strategy."

As they headed to the captain's office, Elise felt the weight of their responsibilities tightening around her. Every step they took unearthed more of The Order's influence and reach. The challenges were mounting, but so were their resolve and resources. As they entered the captain's office, ready to address the new challenges, their determination to dismantle The Order was clearer and more focused than ever. They were not just chasing shadows anymore; they were starting to shine light into the darkest corners of the conspiracy.

The day had taken a turn for the complex for Detectives Elise Bennett and Leo Marquez when an anonymous tip led them to an abandoned warehouse on the industrial outskirts of the city. The tip, received via a secure line to the precinct, claimed that crucial evidence regarding The Order's operations was hidden inside. However, the reality they encountered suggested a possible setup.

Upon arriving at the specified location, the building stood desolate, its large metal doors graffitied and rusted shut. The area was unusually quiet, the only sounds being the distant hum of highway traffic and the occasional clatter of loose metal from the warehouse as the wind picked up. The air was crisp, the fading light casting long shadows that merged with the dark corners of the alleyways.

Elise and Leo approached cautiously, their senses heightened. They circled the building, looking for an entry point or signs of recent activity. Finding a partially opened service door at the back, they drew their weapons, communicating silently through gestures perfected by years of partnership.

Inside, the warehouse was cavernous and dimly lit by shafts of light piercing through broken skylights. Dust particles danced in the beams, creating a ghostly atmosphere. They moved slowly, scanning the area with their flashlights, which cut through the darkness, revealing stacks of wooden crates and old machinery.

"Looks abandoned for years," Leo whispered, his voice echoing slightly in the vast space.

Elise nodded, her flashlight beam settling on a pile of debris that seemed out of place. "Let's check that out."

As they approached, their footsteps disturbing the dust-covered floor, it became evident that the tip might have been a wild goose chase. The pile consisted merely of old, water-damaged boxes filled with moldy paperwork, none of it relevant to their case. There was no sign of recent activity or any evidence related to The Order.

After a thorough search of the area yielded nothing, Elise stepped outside to call in their findings. "This is Bennett. The tip was a bust—no evidence found. Looks like we might have been misled."

Leo, joining her outside, looked around the perimeter, his mind racing with implications. "Could it have been a distraction? Maybe to pull us away from something else?"

"Possibly," Elise replied, her gaze distant. "Or to gauge our response time and resources."

They decided to set up a brief surveillance of the area, suspecting that they might still be observed. As dusk turned to night, they watched from their car, but the hours passed with no sign of movement or interest in the warehouse.

"Time to call it," Elise finally said, her disappointment masked by the calm professionalism she maintained. "Let's get back. We'll need to trace the origin of that tip first thing in the morning."

As they drove back to the precinct, the city's lights blurred past, a stark contrast to the darkness they had just left. The misleading tip was a setback, but both detectives knew that in their line of work, not every lead panned out. What mattered was how quickly they could pivot, reassess, and regain focus on their primary objectives.

Back at their desks, surrounded by the familiar buzz of the precinct, Elise and Leo updated their files, documenting the night's efforts. Despite the lack of results, every detail was crucial, forming part of the larger puzzle they were slowly piecing together.

Tomorrow would bring new challenges, but for now, they had done all they could. The city continued to hold its secrets, and The Order remained a shadowy presence, but Elise and Leo were determined to bring everything into the light. The chase was far from over, and they were ready for whatever lay ahead.

After the misleading tip and a long night of fruitless surveillance, Elise Bennett and Leo Marquez reconvened in the early hours of the morning at the precinct to reassess their strategy. The quiet hum of the office served as a backdrop to their discussion, which centered on the recent series of events that seemed designed more to exhaust their resources and attention than to lead them to concrete evidence.

"Are we playing right into their hands?" Elise mused aloud, looking over the city map dotted with locations they had checked in the past weeks.

Leo leaned back in his chair, rubbing his tired eyes. "It feels like every move we make is being anticipated, or worse, manipulated. Maybe it's time we consider pulling back a bit, changing our approach."

Elise considered this, tapping a pen against her desk. "A strategic withdrawal might give us some room to breathe and see who comes out of the woodwork. We've been pushing hard. Letting up might make them overconfident or careless."

"Do we have enough resources to keep up surveillance on the known locations while appearing to back down?" Leo asked, his brow furrowed in thought.

"We can maintain minimal surveillance, just enough to keep tabs without showing our full hand," Elise replied, starting to outline a potential plan on her notepad. "We'll pull back on the raids and high-profile actions. Keep it quiet, keep it simple."

"That could work," Leo agreed, nodding slowly. "We'll need to be careful about our communications, too. Assume that anything could be intercepted. Maybe even use that to our advantage, feed them some misinformation."

Elise smiled faintly, a spark of strategic satisfaction in her eyes. "Exactly. Let's start using secure lines more often, and maybe drop a few false leads in the mix, see if they take the bait."

The rest of the morning was spent in detailed planning, setting up the parameters of their new approach. They decided to involve only a small, trusted part of their team in this phase of the operation to maintain the integrity and secrecy of their strategy.

Later that day, Elise briefed Captain Roberts on their decision. In his office, surrounded by the quiet buzz of police radios and phone calls, she laid out their revised strategy.

"We're adjusting our tactics," Elise explained. "The recent leads haven't panned out, and we suspect they might be decoys. We're planning to reduce visible activity, which should help us draw out genuine movements by The Order."

Captain Roberts listened intently, nodding along before responding. "Sounds like a solid plan. Keep me updated on any shifts in their pattern. We don't want to give them too much room, but I agree that this might force their hand."

With the captain's approval, Elise and Leo set their plan into motion. Over the next few weeks, their outward pursuit slowed, but their vigilance remained high. They monitored communications and watched for any unusual activity at the previously identified locations.

This period of apparent inactivity was frustrating but necessary, giving them a chance to cleanse their operation of any potential leaks or tracking The Order might have placed. It was a game of patience and nerve, waiting to see who would make the next move.

As they sat in their office late one evening, reviewing the lack of activity, Leo let out a long breath. "It's quiet. Too quiet."

Elise nodded, her eyes still on the screen showing live feeds from their surveillance cameras. "It is. But this is part of the process. We've shaken the tree. Now we wait for something to fall out."

This strategic withdrawal was a new kind of operation, one not defined by the swift action of raids or interrogations but by the silent, watchful waiting of a chess game where each player hides their true intentions. For Elise and Leo, the quiet was not a sign of inactivity but the deep breath before the plunge into the storm they knew was coming.

Chapter 17
The Puppeteer's Game

Elise Bennett and Leo Marquez were gathered around a cluttered desk in the digital forensics lab, staring at a computer screen displaying the latest message intercepted from a suspected member of The Order. The message was cryptic, filled with obscure references and coded language that seemed designed to thwart easy interpretation.

"Any luck making sense of this?" Leo asked, his eyes squinted in concentration as he read through the message again.

"Not much. It's like they're deliberately using a mix of historical and mythological references to encode their communications," Elise responded, her voice tinged with frustration. She pointed at a particular line in the message. "Here, for example, they mention 'the vessel of dawn.' That could be symbolic, or it could be literal—a person, a place, maybe even an event."

Erica, the lead digital analyst, chimed in from her position at the computer. "I've been running some of the phrases through databases of historical and literary sources. Some of these terms come up in ancient texts related to astronomical events and old mythologies."

"Could they be planning something timed with an astronomical event?" Leo speculated, his brows furrowing. "Like an eclipse or a rare planetary alignment?"

"It's possible," Erica said, nodding. She clicked through several windows, pulling up a star chart on the screen. "There's a lunar eclipse due in about three weeks. It lines up with some of the other dates mentioned in earlier messages we've decoded."

Elise leaned closer, examining the star chart. "That might be our window then. They could be planning a major event to coincide with the eclipse.

It fits their pattern—using significant celestial events to amplify the perceived power of their rituals."

Leo drummed his fingers on the desk, thinking aloud. "We need to figure out where this 'vessel of dawn' fits into all this. It's mentioned several times. It could be crucial to understanding their plan."

"I'll dig deeper into the reference," Erica offered, already typing rapidly. "I'll check against all known cultural and mythological databases. Anything that pops up consistently across different sources might give us a clue."

"Good," Elise said, standing up to stretch her legs, her mind racing with possibilities. "While Erica works on that, let's revisit the surveillance data from the last few weeks. We might have overlooked something in light of this new information."

Leo nodded and pulled up another database on a second screen. "Let's cross-reference the dates mentioned in these messages with our surveillance logs. If they were preparing for something big, there might be increased activity at some of their known locations."

The next hour was spent in intense concentration, with only the click of the mouse and the occasional murmur between them as they sifted through data. Every so often, Erica would update them with findings from her searches, adding pieces to the ever-complex puzzle.

"Here's something," Erica suddenly announced, breaking the silence. "The phrase 'vessel of dawn' appears in an ancient Greek ritual text, referring to a ceremonial object used to invoke the goddess of the hunt, associated with the moon."

Elise perked up, turning back to the screen. "That could be it. They might be planning to use or unveil a specific object during the eclipse— something they believe will grant them power or success."

"That makes sense," Leo agreed, his tone cautious but optimistic. "We need to keep pulling on that thread. Find out what this object could be, where it might be now, and what they plan to do with it."

As they wrapped up their session in the lab, the team felt a renewed sense of urgency. They were not just decoding messages; they were uncovering a blueprint for what could be a significant and potentially dangerous event. The next steps were clear: continue to decode, surveil, and prepare to intervene if necessary. With each decoded word and confirmed suspicion, they moved closer to preventing whatever The Order had planned for the night of the eclipse.

In the dim light of the interrogation room, Elise Bennett sat across from Marcus Eldridge, the enigmatic leader of The Order, whose influence seemed to extend beyond the bars that currently confined him. The room was stark, the only sounds the hum of the fluorescent lights and the distant echo of footsteps in the precinct's hallways.

Marcus sat with an unsettling calm, his hands folded neatly on the table, his gaze fixed on Elise with an intensity that was almost palpable. Elise, maintaining her composure, prepared to navigate the verbal chess game that she knew this interrogation would become.

"Marcus, we've been uncovering more about your plans," Elise began, her voice steady. "The upcoming eclipse, the rituals, the so-called 'vessel of dawn.' It's clear you've set something in motion that we are very close to disrupting."

Marcus smiled thinly, his demeanor unshaken. "Detective Bennett, your efforts are commendable, but as always, you see only the surface of a much deeper current."

Elise leaned forward slightly, her eyes never leaving his. "Then enlighten me. What is the depth of this current? Help me understand why you would endanger so many lives for what appears to be nothing more than an elaborate delusion."

"You misunderstand the nature of belief and power, Detective," Marcus replied smoothly. "What we harness is as old as civilization itself. The alignment, the vessel—these are but tools to achieve what humanity has always sought: transcendence."

Elise resisted the urge to glance at the one-way mirror to her left, behind which she knew Leo and other members of her team were watching. "And the cost? The lives disrupted, the families torn apart? Is transcendence worth that price?"

"There is always a price, Elise. Progress demands sacrifice. You, as a servant of the law, should understand that better than anyone," Marcus countered, his use of her first name a deliberate ploy to unnerve.

Elise didn't bite, keeping her tone even. "Your philosophy justifies harm for gains that are, at best, hypothetical. We deal with realities, Marcus, not fantasies. And the reality is, you're here, your network is unraveling, and your plans, whatever they are, will be thwarted."

Marcus's expression hardened for a fleeting moment before he regained his composure. "Perhaps. But consider this, Detective: every step you take to counter us only brings you closer to understanding our truth. Whether you admit it or not, you are becoming a part of the very current you seek to disrupt."

Elise paused, processing his words, recognizing the tactic for what it was—an attempt to sow doubt and discord. She stood, her chair scraping slightly against the floor. "Thank you for your time, Marcus. Rest assured, any current I am a part of leads towards justice, not chaos."

As she stepped out of the interrogation room, Elise felt the weight of Marcus's words, but they did not sway her. Instead, they solidified her resolve. She met Leo outside, his expression questioning.

"Anything useful?" he asked.

"Possibly. His confidence could be indicative of plans still in motion, or it could be bluster designed to mislead us," Elise responded, her mind already turning over her next moves.

"We'll keep digging, Elise. He's in a cell, but we're not taking any chances," Leo reassured her, his loyalty and support unwavering.

As they walked back to their office, Elise felt the complexity of the game they were engaged in. It wasn't just a battle of wits and wills with Marcus and The Order; it was a challenge to maintain their moral and tactical integrity in the face of a shadowy ideology that threatened to engulf all it touched. This psychological duel was far from over, but Elise was prepared to see it through to the end, driven by a commitment to protect and serve, grounded in reality, not shadowy beliefs.

Back at the precinct, Elise Bennett and Leo Marquez huddled with their core team in a strategy session designed to not just respond to The Order's moves but to preempt them.

"We've been reactive for too long," Elise started, her eyes scanning the room, meeting those of her colleagues who had been through the thick of this with her. "It's time we set a trap of our own. We know they're planning something for the lunar eclipse. We can use this event to our advantage."

Leo chimed in, organizing their thoughts into a plan. "Based on what we've gathered from the journal and the emails, their ritual requires a specific setting and artifacts. We control the setting, we control the outcome."

"What do you suggest?" asked Detective Harris, leaning forward, his interest piqued.

"We know the location they've planned to use. We set it up as if we haven't interfered. Surveillance everywhere, but hidden. We let them think they're proceeding as planned," Leo explained.

Elise nodded, elaborating further. "We replace the 'vessel of dawn' with a duplicate. Erica, you said the tech team could rig a fake that looks identical?"

"Yes, we can," Erica confirmed from the side of the room, her laptop open in front of her. "It'll take a bit of time to make it convincing, but we can have it ready before the eclipse."

"And I assume we'll be using the original for leverage?" Detective Reynolds asked, a hint of skepticism in his voice about the ethical implications.

"Exactly," Elise replied. "We hold onto the real artifact. If all goes as planned, when they attempt their ritual with the duplicate, it'll disrupt their expectations. Psychological impact could be significant. It could lead to disarray within their ranks."

"Could this backfire?" asked another team member, Officer Martinez, concerned about the potential for escalation.

"It's a risk," Leo admitted, "but any large-scale operation carries risks. Our presence will be masked but ready to intervene. We'll have tactical units on standby, out of sight, prepared for any sign of trouble."

Elise took a moment to ensure her next instructions were clear. "We need absolute secrecy about this operation. Only people in this room are to know the full plan. Everyone else on the ground follows standard protocol for a surveillance mission. No hints about the intervention."

"What about Marcus?" Harris posed the inevitable question. "He's still a link to them somehow. Any chance he could tip them off from inside?"

"We keep him in the dark, as usual. Strictly no visits, no calls, no communication with the outside that isn't monitored," Elise firmly stated. "We also plant the idea that we've been too busy with false leads to focus on the eclipse. Feed a bit of misinformation about our resources being stretched thin."

"Let's prepare detailed briefs for the units involved. I want everyone to know their role inside and out," Leo added, always focused on operational details.

As the meeting wrapped up, the team felt a rare sense of control over the situation. They were no longer merely reacting but actively manipulating the circumstances to create an advantage. It was a complex plan, requiring precision and coordination, but the stakes were too high for half-measures.

"We set the stage," Elise concluded, her tone resolute as the team dispersed to set the plan in motion. "Let's turn their game against them."

The next few days were a blur of preparations. As the lunar eclipse approached, tension mounted, but so did the readiness of the team. Elise and Leo oversaw every detail, ensuring that the trap was set perfectly, unaware of how the night would unfold but certain that they were ready to face whatever came.

The night of the lunar eclipse had arrived, and with it, an air of expectancy hung around the team assembled by Elise Bennett and Leo Marquez. They had chosen the museum, a neoclassical building with sprawling grounds that The Order had intended to use for their climactic ritual. The museum's current exhibit on astronomical phenomena made it an ironically perfect venue for their operation.

Elise and Leo positioned themselves in the museum's control room, a hub of monitors linked to cameras discreetly placed around and inside the building. The team was in place, everyone aware of their roles in the impending sting operation.

"Everything's set. How are you holding up?" Leo asked, glancing at Elise as she surveyed the screens, her expression a mask of concentration.

"We've planned as much as we can. Now it's up to how they play their hand," Elise replied, her voice steady despite the adrenaline she felt coursing through her veins.

As the eclipse began, the museum grounds remained eerily quiet. Then, slowly, figures cloaked in dark robes began to converge on the site. The cameras picked up their cautious movements as they made their way to the designated ritual area, unaware of the eyes watching them.

"Here they come. Just as expected," Leo murmured, his hand hovering over the radio, ready to give the signal if things escalated.

The Order's members assembled around the fake 'vessel of dawn,' placed exactly where the original had been intended to be. The leader, a tall figure in an ornate mask, stepped forward, raising his arms as he began to chant in a resonant voice. The others followed suit, their voices rising in a strange, melodic cadence.

Elise watched, her focus absolute. "Wait for it. Let them commit fully."

The ritual continued, the chanting growing louder as the eclipse reached its peak. Then, at the moment of total coverage, the leader reached for the 'vessel,' his movements deliberate. As he lifted it, expecting a surge of power or a sign, nothing happened. Confusion rippled through the group, their chanting faltering.

"Now," Elise said into her radio, her voice low but clear. "Move in."

Teams of officers emerged from their hidden positions, converging on the ritual site swiftly and efficiently. The members of The Order, caught off guard and without their anticipated supernatural protection, offered little resistance.

Leo coordinated the arrests, speaking rapidly into the radio as he directed teams to secure the area and detain the Order's members. "Make sure everyone is accounted for. Check for any additional artifacts they might have brought with them."

As the operation wound down, Elise stepped out from the control room to survey the scene. The members of The Order were being led away in handcuffs, their robes and masks stark against the police lights.

Leo joined her, a slight smile of relief on his face. "It worked, Elise. We got them."

"We did," Elise acknowledged, allowing herself a moment to feel the weight of their success. "But this is just a part of it. We need to ensure they don't regroup."

As they watched the last of the members being escorted to the police vehicles, Elise felt a mix of satisfaction and wariness. Tonight had been a victory, but the war against The Order's ideology and its roots in the city was far from over.

"We'll debrief back at the precinct. Good work tonight, Leo," Elise said, turning to head back inside.

"Thanks, Elise. You too. Let's go home," Leo replied, following her as they left the museum grounds behind, the eclipse receding and the night gradually reclaiming its normalcy. The game had indeed been played, and for now, they had won. But the game, as always, was bound to evolve.

Chapter 18
The Secret Library

In the cool, early morning hours following the successful operation at the museum, Detectives Elise Bennett and Leo Marquez convened in a small, cluttered conference room at the precinct to assess the aftermath and plan their next steps.

Leo was updating a large whiteboard with names and details, connecting them with lines to form a clearer picture of The Order's remaining structure. "We got most of them last night," he said, stepping back to review the information. "But there are still a few key players at large, and we need to find out how they'll react."

Elise, sipping her coffee, nodded in agreement. "The operation was a success, but it's not the end. We disrupted their ritual, yes, but we also pushed them into a corner. They'll be desperate now, possibly more dangerous."

"What about the items we recovered?" Leo asked, referring to the various artifacts and documents that had been seized during the raid.

"They're being cataloged and examined by forensics. One item, in particular, caught my attention," Elise responded, pulling out a photo from a file and handing it to Leo. It showed an intricately carved wooden box with symbols similar to those in the journal they had previously recovered.

Leo examined the photo. "This looks ancient. Any idea what it contains?"

"The team is still working on opening it safely. It's locked, and there seems to be a mechanism that could potentially damage the contents if forced," Elise explained.

The door to the conference room opened, and Captain Roberts walked in, his expression serious. "Good work last night, both of you. How are we standing?"

Elise gave him a brief summary, then added, "We're planning to dig deeper into the documents we found. There's a reference to a location we haven't checked yet — something they called 'the secret library.' It could be metaphorical, but given their penchant for drama, it might be a real place."

"Do we have any leads on where this library could be?" Captain Roberts asked, looking between Elise and Leo.

"Not yet," Leo replied. "But the documents mention several older properties that haven't come up in our searches before. We're cross-referencing them with city records to see if anything stands out."

Captain Roberts nodded. "Make that your priority. If there's a central hub we haven't cracked yet, it could give us the rest of what we need to completely dismantle their operations."

As the meeting concluded, Elise and Leo set to work, poring over maps and property records, searching for any clue that might indicate the location of the so-called secret library. They made a list of potential sites, historical buildings that had been overlooked or were under the radar.

"Let's split these up," Elise suggested. "I'll take the northern sites, you take the southern. Anything that looks remotely like it could be used by The Order, we take a closer look."

"Got it," Leo agreed, gathering his notes and preparing to head out.

As they left the precinct to follow their respective leads, the city was waking up. The streets were filling with the early bustle of commuters and the day promised more discoveries. Elise felt the familiar thrill of the chase, tempered by the weight of responsibility. The pieces of the puzzle were slowly fitting together, and each step brought them closer to the heart of The Order's mysteries. As she drove towards her first location, her determination was clear: unravel the secrets, find the library, and end the game once and for all.

Elise Bennett drove through the winding streets of the older part of the city, her eyes scanning the aging facades of buildings that had stood witness to the city's evolving history. Based on the clues sifted from the documents recovered from the museum, she was searching for any property that matched the descriptions linked to what The Order referred to as "the secret library."

Stopping outside an old Victorian house that now stood empty, Elise felt a tug of intuition. The building, with its overgrown garden and boarded-up windows, had a secretive air about it that fit the profile from the cryptic references in the documents.

She called Leo on her cell. "I think I've found something. It's the old Hartford place on Willow Street. Matches the description from one of the ledgers. I'm going in to take a closer look."

"Be careful," Leo's voice crackled through the speaker. "I'm about fifteen minutes out but heading your way now."

Elise approached the house, her senses heightened. The front door was locked, but she found a way in through a side window that wasn't fully secured. Inside, the air was musty, filled with the scent of old books and dust. She flashed her light around, the beam catching on rows and rows of shelves crammed with books, some so old their spines were cracked and faded.

She stepped further into the room, her flashlight illuminating the vast collection. "This has to be it, Leo. It's a library, alright. Looks like it hasn't been touched in years."

Moving deeper, Elise noticed that the books weren't just old—they were rare. Many dealt with esoteric and occult topics, consistent with The Order's interests. As she scanned the titles, she spotted several volumes that were listed in the journal as key texts for their doctrines.

Elise heard a noise at the door and turned to see Leo entering, his expression a mix of relief and curiosity as he looked around. "This is incredible," he said, joining her among the shelves. "It's like stepping back in time."

They split up to search the room more thoroughly. Elise found a hidden panel behind a false wall on one side of the library. With effort, she slid it open, revealing a small, secret room. Inside, there was a desk with various artifacts, papers, and another set of books that seemed even more personal and meticulously kept.

Leo came over to help examine the new find. "What do you make of this?" he asked, picking up one of the artifacts, a small, intricately carved box that resembled the descriptions of items used in their rituals.

"It's part of their core," Elise replied, examining a map laid out on the desk that detailed other locations around the city. "These are planning documents, Leo. It looks like this place was more than just a library; it was a hub for their leadership."

The discovery was significant, and they knew they needed to preserve everything exactly as it was for the forensic team to analyze. Elise took photos and then stepped back, her mind already racing ahead to the implications of their find.

"This could be the break we needed," she said, her voice steady despite the excitement. "With this evidence, we can not only prove their activities but potentially unravel their entire network."

Leo nodded in agreement, looking around the secret room with a sense of awe. "Let's get the team in here to secure everything. This is a big win, Elise."

As they left the house to wait for the forensic team, the weight of their discovery hung between them, a mixture of triumph and the sobering realization of how deep and dark the rabbit hole went. They had uncovered a vital part of The Order's world—a hidden library where plans were made and doctrines were kept. Now, it was time to use this knowledge to end The Order's game once and for all.

After the forensic team had swept through the secret library, ensuring that every book, document, and artifact was carefully cataloged and preserved, Elise Bennett and Leo Marquez returned to examine the contents more thoroughly. They were joined by Dr. Harold Finch, the consultant who had helped them interpret historical and esoteric texts previously.

The room was quiet, save for the rustling of pages and occasional murmurs as they delved deeper into the ancient knowledge that had been hoarded in this hidden room. Each document, each book, seemed to peel back another layer of The Order's mysteries.

"This is fascinating," Dr. Finch remarked, his eyes wide as he handled a particularly old manuscript. "This text is a rare alchemical treatise that dates back to the 17th century. It's incredibly well preserved."

Elise, who was examining a series of maps and notes, looked up. "Harold, do any of these texts give us more insight into what The Order was planning? Anything that could be their next move?"

Dr. Finch flipped through another book, stopping to read certain passages more carefully. "Many of these writings discuss transformation and rebirth through alignment with celestial events. It's clear they were not just dabbling in these concepts but were deeply committed to them."

Leo, scanning through some of the personal letters found in the desk, added, "There are several references here to 'ascending to the next plane of existence.' They were planning something big, something permanent."

"Any indication of when?" Elise asked, her voice tense with the urgency of their investigation.

Dr. Finch pointed to a line in the manuscript he was reading. "Here, it mentions the 'culmination of the grand cycle' during the upcoming solar eclipse. That's less than a month away."

Elise's eyes narrowed. "A solar eclipse... that could be what they've been building up to all this time. It fits the pattern."

Leo stood up, stretching his back. "We need to put together a timeline of these events and cross-reference them with known Order activities. If we can predict their endpoint, we might be able to stop them before they start."

Dr. Finch nodded, carefully placing the manuscript down on the desk. "I'll help compile the data. The historical significance alone is enormous, but right now, the immediate threat takes precedence."

As they worked together, the puzzle began to form a clearer picture. Each piece of ancient wisdom, each cryptic diary entry, added to their understanding of The Order's philosophical and potentially cataclysmic goals.

"This isn't just about history or philosophy anymore," Elise said, her voice low. "It's about preventing a potential disaster."

Leo looked over at her, his expression somber. "We'll stop them, Elise. We've got the best team, and now we've got their playbook."

They continued working into the evening, the room illuminated by the soft glow of desk lamps, surrounded by relics of a darker age. The weight of responsibility was palpable, but so was the drive to protect the unsuspecting city from a shadow that had grown in its midst, unseen but deeply felt.

As they finally called it a night, Elise paused at the door, taking one last look at the room that had yielded so many secrets. "Tomorrow, we bring this to the task force. Then we end this."

Leo nodded in agreement, fatigue etching his features but his resolve unwavering. "Let's bring this chapter to a close."

They left the library, the door locking behind them with a click that sounded like a period at the end of a long, complicated sentence. But the story was far from over, and they knew the final chapters were yet to be written.

In the quiet of the early morning, before the bustle of the precinct filled the air, Elise Bennett sat in her office surrounded by the scattered documents and books from the secret library. The pieces were coming together, the narrative of The Order's long-planned event becoming clearer with each document they decoded.

Leo Marquez knocked and entered, a coffee cup in each hand. He placed one on her desk before sitting down. "Thought you could use one of these," he said, indicating the coffee.

"Thanks," Elise replied, accepting the cup and taking a sip. She then gestured to the map spread out on her desk, marked with various dates and locations. "Look at this. All the lines converge at the upcoming solar eclipse. Whatever The Order is planning, it's big, and it's been decades in the making."

Leo leaned over the map, tracing the lines with his finger. "So, we think they're planning to enact whatever this 'grand cycle' is then?"

"Exactly," Elise confirmed. "And every ritual, every gathering that we've disrupted so far, was just a precursor to this."

"So, what's our play?" Leo asked, his brow furrowed in concern.

"We prevent it," Elise stated firmly. "We use everything we've learned, set up surveillance at the identified locations, and prepare for a major intervention."

Leo nodded, his expression turning resolute. "We'll need to coordinate with other agencies, make sure we have enough manpower on the ground."

Elise picked up the phone, dialing the number of their task force leader. As she waited for the call to connect, she looked up at Leo. "We also need to inform the mayor's office. If this is as big as we think, the city needs to be prepared for any fallout."

The conversation on the phone was brief but to the point. Elise laid out their findings and received the go-ahead to proceed with their plans. After hanging up, she turned to Leo. "It's all hands on deck now. I'll brief the team in an hour. I want everyone to know their role down to the smallest detail."

Leo stood, ready to mobilize. "I'll get the operational units ready. We'll make sure this doesn't go off as they plan."

As they walked to the briefing room, Elise felt the weight of their task. They were not just dealing with a criminal group but a cult with deep roots and a dangerous vision for the future.

The briefing room was filled with the hum of urgent conversations as other detectives and officers prepared for the briefing. Elise stepped to the front, clearing her throat to silence the room. She outlined the situation, the evidence from the secret library, and their strategy for the eclipse.

"The Order has planned this for decades," Elise explained to the room. "They believe what they are doing is right, that it will change the world. Our job is to ensure the safety of the public and prevent any harm they might cause."

The team listened intently, their faces a mix of determination and concern. After the briefing, they dispersed to finalize preparations, each person aware of the stakes.

Leo lingered behind, approaching Elise as the room cleared. "You did well, Elise. We're as ready as we'll ever be."

Elise nodded, her gaze steady. "Thanks, Leo. Whatever happens, we'll face it together."

As they left the briefing room, the first light of dawn was breaking over the city. The day ahead would be long and might very well be pivotal in the history of their city. Elise and Leo, fortified by their resolve and the strength of their team, were ready to face whatever The Order intended. The realization of their responsibility was profound, but so was their commitment to end this threat once and for all.

Chapter 19
The Fifth Victim

On a chilly morning that promised rain, Detectives Elise Bennett and Leo Marquez were called to a secluded section of the city park, a place rarely frequented by the usual joggers and dog walkers. The scene they arrived at was cordoned off by police tape, with uniformed officers keeping the growing crowd of curious onlookers at bay.

As Elise and Leo ducked under the tape, they were met by Detective Harris, who looked unusually pale. "What's the situation, Harris?" Elise asked, noting his grim expression.

"We found another one, Elise," Harris replied, his voice low. "Just like the others, but this time there's something different."

Leo's brow furrowed in concern. "Different how?"

Harris turned, leading them toward the crime scene. "You'll need to see for yourselves. It's unsettling."

They followed him to a clearing where the body lay covered by a stark white sheet. As they approached, the forensic analyst, Dr. Simmons, stood up from where he had been crouching next to the body. He nodded grimly at Elise and Leo.

"Detectives," Dr. Simmons began as he pulled back the sheet, "like the previous victims, the cause of death appears to be related to a ritualistic act. However, this time the victim's markings are more elaborate, and there's an inscription."

Elise stepped closer, examining the scene. Carved into the ground around the body were symbols and what appeared to be a phrase in a foreign language. "Have we identified the victim?"

"Not yet," Dr. Simmons answered. "But based on the attire and personal effects, it looks like he was a scholar, possibly someone with a background in theology or ancient languages."

Leo knelt beside the body, inspecting the symbols. "This is sophisticated, and chillingly methodical. Any idea what the inscription says?"

"We're working on it," Dr. Simmons replied. "It's not a language commonly seen. We've sent images to a linguistics expert at the university. Should have something soon."

Elise stood back up, her mind racing with the implications of this new victim. "This changes the pattern. The other victims were all connected to The Order, but in a more peripheral way. A scholar, especially one who might understand their rituals or ideologies, suggests a deeper connection."

Leo looked up at her, concern etching his features deeper. "Or a warning to others who might interfere or possess knowledge that could threaten them."

Elise turned to Harris. "I want a list of known associates of the victim as soon as we have an ID. And check any recent academic publications or lectures that might be linked to this... whatever this is."

Harris nodded, taking notes. "Will do. I'll also review security footage from the surrounding area and speak to park personnel. Whoever did this took a risk by leaving the body in such an accessible place."

As the team worked, Elise pulled Leo aside. "We need to be careful, Leo. This feels like an escalation, a message not just to us but to anyone who might oppose The Order."

Leo's expression was grim but determined. "We'll ramp up our efforts. Increase surveillance on all known Order locations and double-check our intel. If they're getting bolder, it means they're either desperate or close to achieving whatever they're planning."

Elise nodded, her resolve hardening. "Let's get back to the precinct. We have a lot of work ahead of us, and I want to be there when Simmons gets the translation of that inscription."

As they left the scene, the weight of the morning's discovery lingered heavily on them both. This case was evolving, growing darker and more complex by the day, and now more than ever, they needed to stay one step ahead to prevent further loss of life.

The precinct was a flurry of activity as Elise Bennett and Leo Marquez returned from the unsettling scene at the park. Their immediate task was to piece together the cryptic clues left with the fifth victim, hoping to uncover a lead that would direct them closer to the perpetrator or perpetrators.

Upon their arrival, they headed straight to the lab where the linguistics expert, Dr. Amelia Foster, was already at work deciphering the inscription found at the crime scene. The air in the lab was tense, charged with the urgency of their task.

Elise approached Dr. Foster, who looked up from her desk strewn with ancient language dictionaries and digital images of the inscription. "Dr. Foster, any progress?" Elise asked, her voice a mix of hope and impatience.

Dr. Foster nodded, pushing her glasses up her nose. "Yes, Detective Bennett. The inscription is in an archaic form of Aramaic. It's quite rare and not easy to translate quickly. But I've managed to make some headway."

"And?" Leo interjected, stepping closer to examine the photographs of the symbols and text laid out on the table.

"The text is a warning," Dr. Foster began, her tone serious. "It speaks of a retribution for those who betray the sacred secrets. It's phrased like a curse or a prophecy. Quite ominous."

Elise exchanged a glance with Leo. "Could the victim have been involved with The Order and then tried to leave or expose them?"

"It's a strong possibility," Leo replied. "This could be a message to anyone inside the group thinking of doing the same."

Dr. Foster handed Elise a printed translation of the inscription. "I'll continue to work on this, see if there's more context I can uncover that might be helpful."

"Thank you, Dr. Foster. Keep us posted on anything else you find," Elise said as she took the translation.

With the new information in hand, Elise and Leo left the lab and headed to their office to regroup and plan their next steps. The precinct buzzed around them, every officer and detective driven by a shared urgency to solve the string of disturbing crimes.

In their office, Elise spread out the translation on the desk alongside the map of the city, marking the locations of all known activities and members of The Order. "We need to look at this from every angle. If this is indeed an internal message, then the victim must have had significant knowledge about The Order's operations. Perhaps even records or documents that could lead us to the next potential target or gathering."

Leo leaned over the map, tracing routes and connections with his finger. "We should also consider increasing protection for others who might be at risk. Any former members, known dissenters within the group, or anyone who has left recently under suspicious circumstances."

Elise nodded, her mind racing with the implications of their findings. "I'll get Harris and the team to start cross-referencing the victim's known associates with our list of Order members. We need to identify anyone who fits the profile and might be in danger."

The rest of the day was spent coordinating with various departments, organizing protection details, and combing through evidence with the new clues in mind. The work was meticulous and exhaustive, but every piece of information added to their understanding of The Order's twisted ethos and methods.

As evening approached and the precinct began to quiet down, Elise took a moment to reflect on the day's revelations. The pieces were slowly fitting together, but the full picture was still disturbingly unclear. With each victim, The Order revealed a bit more of its dark nature, but the depth of its influence and the reach of its roots were yet to be fully uncovered.

Determined and resolute, Elise and Leo prepared for the long night ahead, knowing that their adversary was both cunning and cruel. But they were driven by a relentless pursuit of justice, fueled by the realization that they were not just solving crimes but potentially saving lives from a hidden, pervasive evil.

After a long day of digging through new leads and coordinating with different departments, Elise Bennett and Leo Marquez found themselves late in the evening in the quiet of the precinct's rooftop garden, a place they often came to think and regroup away from the chaos below.

The city lights twinkled around them, a stark contrast to the darkness they were trying to unravel. Elise leaned against the railing, her eyes distant but thoughtful.

Leo broke the silence, his voice carrying a weight of concern. "Do you ever wonder if we're really making a difference, Elise? With each case we close, it feels like two more spring up in its place."

Elise turned to look at him, her expression somber yet resolute. "I do wonder, Leo. But then I think about the lives we've saved, the people we've helped. We may not be able to stop every evil, but we can at least make it harder for them to operate."

Leo nodded, appreciating her steadfastness. "You're right, of course. It's just that this case, The Order... it's like a hydra. Cut off one head, and another appears."

"It's a tough battle," Elise agreed, pushing off from the railing to pace slightly. "But think about today. We learned more about their beliefs, their methods. Every piece of the puzzle we put together is a step closer to stopping them for good."

Leo watched her, admiring her determination. "I guess it's about the small victories, isn't it? Each clue uncovered, each victim remembered."

"Exactly," Elise said, stopping her pacing to face him. "And tonight, we reflect on those victories, small as they may be. We regroup, and tomorrow, we go back into the fray even stronger."

Their conversation drifted then to lighter topics, a necessary reprieve from the intensity of their work. They discussed plans for the precinct's upcoming community outreach, a project close to both their hearts.

After a while, Elise glanced at her watch and sighed. "We should get back. There's still a lot to prepare for tomorrow."

Leo agreed, and they made their way down to the squad room. The precinct was quieter now, the hustle of the day giving way to the slow, steady rhythm of the night shift.

As they reached her desk, Elise picked up a small photo pinned to her board—a reminder of one of their first big cases together, solved and closed. It served as a silent testament to their partnership and success.

Leo, following her gaze, smiled. "To many more solved cases."

"To many more," Elise echoed, a smile tugging at the corner of her mouth.

They settled back into their work, the earlier conversation a gentle echo in their minds. Despite the challenges, they were united in their mission—driven by the knowledge that every effort they made was a strike against the darkness, a beacon of hope in the night. The work was hard, the hours long, but as they reviewed their notes and planned for the days ahead, there was no place they would rather be, no work they would rather be doing. In the fight against evil, every small victory was a victory indeed, and every day brought them closer to the next one.

Back at the precinct the following morning, Elise Bennett and Leo Marquez were deep in discussion over the latest evidence gathered, when a call came through Elise's phone. She glanced at the caller ID—it was an unknown number, but she had a hunch about who it might be and decided to answer.

"Detective Bennett speaking."

The voice on the other end was cautious but clear. "Detective, you don't know me, but I believe we share a common interest in stopping The Order. I have information that might be useful to you."

Elise's interest piqued, and she motioned for Leo to listen in. "I'm listening. Who am I speaking with?"

"You can call me Alex. I was once part of The Order, but I left. I couldn't stomach where things were heading," the caller revealed, their voice tinged with a mix of fear and determination.

Elise quickly grabbed a notepad, jotting down notes. "Why come forward now, Alex?"

"The death of the fifth victim. I knew him. He was a good man, trying to expose some of the darker aspects of The Order. His death wasn't just a warning to others—it was a sign of how dangerous they've become," Alex explained.

Leo, who had been listening intently, chimed in. "What can you tell us that might help prevent further violence?"

"There's a meeting, a major one, planned soon. It's where they intend to finalize the next phase of their plan. I can give you the details, but I need protection. They know I left, and if they find out I'm talking to you…"

"We'll protect you, Alex," Elise assured quickly. "Let's arrange a time and place to meet, somewhere safe."

After setting up the meeting and hanging up, Elise turned to Leo. "This could be the break we've been waiting for, but we need to be careful. It could also be a setup."

Leo nodded, his expression serious. "We'll take every precaution. Let's get a team together, make sure we're prepared for anything."

Later that day, in a nondescript café, Elise and Leo met with Alex. A young man in his late twenties, Alex looked wary but resolute as he handed over a USB drive containing encrypted files.

"These include details of the meeting, names, locations, everything you'll need to disrupt their plans," Alex said as he slid the drive across the table.

Elise picked up the drive, her gaze steady on Alex. "Why betray them, Alex? Why now?"

Alex looked down, his hands clasped tightly in front of him. "Because I realized that fear was what kept me bound to them. Fear of them, fear of leaving, fear of change. But seeing what they did to my friend, the fifth victim, I realized fear is their weapon. I won't let it control me anymore."

Leo, who had been listening intently, added, "Your courage could save many lives, Alex. We'll do everything we can to keep you safe."

As they wrapped up the meeting, Elise and Leo escorted Alex to a safe house arranged by the department, where he would stay until the upcoming operation was over.

On the drive back to the precinct, Elise turned to Leo. "This alliance, unexpected as it is, might just turn the tide against The Order."

Leo nodded, his gaze fixed on the road ahead. "It's a reminder that change can come from within. Even those who were once on the wrong side can choose to do right."

With Alex's information, they now had a tangible advantage. As the city passed by outside the car windows, both detectives felt the weight of the upcoming operation. It was a chance to significantly weaken The Order, and they were determined to see it through, bolstered by an unexpected alliance that reaffirmed their belief in the possibility of redemption and change.

Chapter 20
Closing In

In the bustling atmosphere of the precinct, Detectives Elise Bennett and Leo Marquez convened in Captain Roberts' office to discuss the expansion of their investigation into The Order. The room was filled with tension, indicative of the crucial phase their case was entering.

Elise laid out a series of photographs and documents on the captain's desk. "With the information Alex provided, we have actionable intel on several more members of The Order who have so far evaded our radar. We need to widen our net."

Captain Roberts, looking over the materials, nodded in agreement. "How expansive are we talking, Bennett?"

"We're not just looking at a few more suspects," Leo chimed in. "This goes beyond the city limits. We have potential links to other groups in neighboring states. It's bigger than we initially thought."

Elise continued, "We need to coordinate with other jurisdictions. Surveillance, raids, the whole spectrum. If we move quickly, we can prevent them from regrouping or going underground."

Captain Roberts leaned back in his chair, processing the information. "That's a major escalation. We'll need clear evidence to support this kind of expansion. The last thing we need is to overreach and come up empty-handed."

"We have the evidence," Elise assured him, pointing to the USB drive Alex had provided. "Financial records, communications, it's all here. Plus, we have Alex's testimony."

"Speaking of which," Leo added, "I've arranged for Alex to meet with the DA's office. He's agreed to testify, provided we can guarantee his safety."

"That's good," Captain Roberts replied. "I'll speak with the DA personally. We'll need every legal advantage we can get if this goes to trial."

Elise picked up a map, spreading it out on the table. It showed several states highlighted in different colors, each representing a known or suspected area of The Order's influence. "Our next step should be setting up task forces in these areas. Each team would be briefed on specific targets and operational protocols."

Captain Roberts stood, indicating he was on board with the plan. "I'll authorize the expansion. Bennett, Marquez, coordinate with the task force leaders. Set up a briefing first thing tomorrow morning."

Leo took notes, his mind already on the logistics. "We'll need to ensure all teams have access to the same intelligence to avoid any gaps in our approach. Seamless communication will be key."

"As will speed," Elise emphasized. "The longer we wait, the more time they have to disappear or worse, execute whatever they're planning next."

Captain Roberts walked them to the door. "I trust you two to handle this. Keep me updated on every step."

As they left the office, Elise and Leo headed straight to the operations center to start organizing the expanded task forces. The room was abuzz with activity, with officers and analysts working at various stations.

"Let's pull in the team leaders. We need everyone on the same page ASAP," Elise instructed, her tone firm but composed.

Leo began making calls, each conversation setting the gears of the vast operation in motion. "We have green light on the expansion. Start pulling your teams together."

Elise, meanwhile, updated the central database with new information for dissemination to all units involved. "Make sure all data is encrypted and secure. No leaks."

As the day wore on, the scale of their task became clearer, but so did their resolve to see it through. This was no longer just about catching a killer or dismantling a local group; it was about eradicating a network that threatened the very fabric of their community.

"This is it, Leo," Elise said as they finally took a moment to breathe. "We're closing in, and this time, we're not just chipping away at the edges. We're going right to the heart."

Leo nodded, his expression one of steely determination. "Let's bring them down, Elise. For good."

Elise Bennett and Leo Marquez found themselves in an unmarked car, the dashboard lit only by the glow of the street lamps outside. They were parked a block away from an apartment complex that had been identified as a possible meeting point for remaining key members of The Order. This was one of several stakeouts set up across the city as part of their expanded operation.

"Are we sure they'll show tonight?" Leo whispered, his eyes not leaving the front entrance of the building.

Elise checked her watch, then glanced at the small screen showing a live feed from a camera they had discreetly installed near the entrance. "According to the last set of communications we intercepted, this is the place. They're becoming more cautious, but they still need to regroup."

Leo sighed, the tension evident in his voice. "It's been a long few days. This could go south fast if they realize they're walking into a surveillance net."

Elise nodded, her focus sharp. "We've got teams ready on standby. If anyone shows up and things turn volatile, we move in. But ideally, we gather as much intel as we can without revealing our hand."

The hours ticked by, with each minute stretching out under the weight of anticipation. They monitored every person who entered or exited the building, but none matched the descriptions of their targets.

Then, a black sedan pulled up to the curb. "That's one of the cars we've been tracking," Leo said, his hand moving toward his radio. "Looks like we might have something."

They watched as two figures exited the vehicle, both matching the descriptions of mid-level Order members known to be close to the leadership. "Got a visual on two possible suspects, male, entering the north entrance," Elise reported quietly into her radio, keeping her eyes on the live feed.

"Confirming visual," came the response from another team member in a different location. "Do you want us to move in?"

"Negative," Elise replied. "Maintain surveillance only. Let's see if they lead us to anyone else."

The two men disappeared into the building, and the team's attention was now fixed on waiting for them to reappear or for someone else to show up. Leo and Elise used this time to review their next steps.

"If they start a meeting, how long do we wait before we intervene?" Leo asked, his gaze still fixed on the building.

"We give it fifteen minutes unless we see a sign of anything immediate or dangerous happening. We need enough to get a warrant for a raid," Elise answered, her mind already running through various scenarios.

As they waited, a sense of unease settled over Leo. "You think they know we're closing in on them?"

Elise considered this. "Possibly. But they're also getting desperate. Desperate people make mistakes."

Before Leo could respond, their attention was drawn back to the screen as three more individuals entered the frame, each one previously identified as a high-priority target. "Looks like it's turning into a significant meet," Elise murmured, her hand reaching for her radio. "We've got three more entering. That's five in total. I think it's time."

"Agreed," Leo said, his voice firm. "Let's prepare to move in. We might not get another chance like this."

Elise gave the signal, and within minutes, police sirens wailed in the distance, converging on the location. The stakeout shifted rapidly into a dynamic operation as teams moved in to secure the building.

The tension of the stakeout broke into the fast-paced action of a raid, each officer and detective moving with precision, driven by the weeks of preparation and investigation that had led them here. For Elise and Leo, this was the culmination of countless hours of work, a crucial turning point in their mission to dismantle The Order from within. As they entered the building, following the tactical team, they were prepared for any confrontation, their resolve as strong as ever.

Inside the apartment building, the atmosphere was thick with tension. Elise Bennett and Leo Marquez, along with a team of tactical officers, moved swiftly and silently up the stairwell towards the apartment where the suspects had gathered. Their steps were measured, the only sounds the muted thuds of their boots and the distant echo of their backup positioning around the perimeter.

As they reached the door, Elise nodded to Leo, who positioned himself on one side, while she took the other. One of the tactical officers placed a listening device at the door. Through the earpiece, Elise could hear low voices, the suspects unaware of the impending breach.

Leo whispered into his radio, confirming positions and readiness. "On my mark," he breathed, his hand signaling the tactical officer with the ram.

The door burst open under the force of the ram, the sound of splintering wood cutting through the murmured conversations inside. The team surged into the apartment, shouting commands that sliced through the confusion.

"Police! Hands where I can see them!"

The suspects, caught by surprise, scrambled. Some raised their hands immediately, while others hesitated, their shock morphing into fear. In the corner of the room, one figure stood out, not moving towards compliance as quickly as the others. It was Malcolm Trent, a high-ranking member of The Order, whose elusive nature had made him a significant target in the investigation.

Elise moved directly towards him, her gun trained steadily. "Malcolm Trent, on your knees, hands on your head!"

Malcolm, his expression a mix of defiance and resignation, slowly knelt, locking eyes with Elise. "Detective Bennett, isn't it? I wondered when we'd finally meet like this."

"You knew we were coming," Elise stated, not as a question but as a fact, her eyes scanning the room while keeping Trent in her peripheral vision.

"Of course," Malcolm replied smoothly, his voice low. "The Order is many things, but naïve isn't one of them. We knew the risks, especially after the museum."

Leo, now cuffing another suspect, kept his attention on the interaction. "Then you know why we're here. The violence, the rituals—it ends tonight."

Malcolm chuckled, a hollow sound that filled the tense room. "You think this is the end? Detective, you're merely at the edge of understanding. The Order is more than its ceremonies and its... sacrifices."

Elise stepped closer, her stance firm. "Then enlighten me. What are we missing?"

Malcolm's gaze hardened. "A vision of a new order, Detective. One that transcends your laws and your moralities. You can arrest us, yes, but ideas? They are immortal."

"You're talking about ideas that kill, that terrorize," Elise shot back. "Ideas that left families mourning. There's nothing transcendent about that."

As they spoke, the other officers secured the room, leading handcuffed suspects out and beginning to search for documents and other evidence. Leo approached Elise, his voice a low murmur. "We've got them, Elise. Let's wrap this up."

Elise nodded, her gaze never leaving Malcolm as another officer stepped forward to cuff him. "You'll have your chance to explain your 'vision' to a judge."

Malcolm stood, the officer holding him firmly. "Detective Bennett, Detective Marquez," he said, a smirk touching his lips despite the circumstances. "This is far from over. Remember, ideas do not bleed."

As Malcolm was led out of the apartment, Elise felt a mix of triumph and the heavy weight of responsibility. They had struck a significant blow against The Order tonight, but his words lingered uncomfortably in her mind.

Outside, as they walked back to their car, Leo glanced at Elise. "What do you think he meant by that?"

Elise considered, her expression thoughtful. "That even with the leaders caught, the ideology survives. We've got more work to do, Leo. More than just arrests."

As they drove away from the scene, the city around them seemed quieter, but beneath that quiet, Elise knew the echoes of Malcolm's words would stir them to remain vigilant. The night had brought a victory, but the battle, it seemed, was far from over.

Back at the precinct, Elise Bennett and Leo Marquez gathered in the strategy room with key members of their task force. The walls were lined with maps and photos, each marked with crucial information about The Order's known activities and remaining hideouts. The air was charged with a sense of urgency as they prepared for what they hoped would be the final confrontation with The Order.

Elise stood at the front of the room, pointing to a map with several locations highlighted. "We've taken down a significant part of their network, but the core group is still out there, likely planning their next move. Based on the intelligence we gathered from Malcolm Trent and the documents seized last night, we believe we've identified their last operational base."

Leo added, flipping through a dossier. "It's located in an old industrial complex on the outskirts of the city. Surveillance has shown increased activity there over the past few days. It's secluded, which makes it ideal for their purposes but also gives us an advantage."

A detective from the tactical unit, Detective Gomez, spoke up. "What's the approach? Full raid?"

Elise nodded. "Yes, but with precision. We can't afford a heavy-handed approach that might result in unnecessary risk or damage. We'll use a two-pronged strategy."

Leo took over, detailing the tactical plan. "First, we'll continue with the surveillance, keep a close eye on everyone entering and leaving the complex. We need to confirm that no civilians are inside. Second, we're going in with SWAT for a swift, clean operation designed to take them by surprise. Timing is critical."

Detective Gomez looked over the plans. "Do we have an entry point picked out?"

"Yes," Leo responded, pointing to a blueprint of the building. "There are two main entrances. Team A will breach the front, while Team B will cover the rear. We'll have snipers in place as a precaution."

Elise looked around the room, her gaze meeting those of her team members. "This is it—the final push. I need everyone sharp and focused. Any questions?"

A younger detective raised his hand. "What's the ROE, Detective Bennett?"

"Rules of engagement are simple: defend yourselves and the team, but every action must be measured and necessary. We want to end this with as little violence as possible," Elise clarified, her tone firm but calm.

Leo chimed in, "Remember, many of these people are deeply indoctrinated. They might not surrender easily. Be prepared for anything."

The room fell silent as the weight of their task settled on everyone's shoulders. Elise took a deep breath, her expression resolute. "We've all worked hard to get to this point. It's been a long road, and I know it's taken its toll on all of us. But tonight, we have a chance to close this chapter for good. Let's make sure we do it right."

As the meeting adjourned, the team members began their final preparations. Weapons were checked, protective gear was fitted, and radios were tested. Elise and Leo stayed behind, reviewing every detail of the operation.

"Think this will be the end of it?" Leo asked quietly, as they were about to leave the room.

Elise paused, considering his question. "Whether it's the end or not, we're making sure it's a significant blow. They won't recover easily from this."

With a nod of agreement, Leo and Elise left the strategy room. They walked down the precinct hallways, each step echoing slightly, a reminder of the path they had walked together. As they stepped into the evening air, heading towards their vehicles, the setting sun cast long shadows behind them, mirroring the long reach of the journey they had undertaken. Tonight, they hoped, would bring an end to the shadow that had loomed over their city for too long.

Chapter 21
Final Puzzle

In the aftermath of the successful raid on the industrial complex, which had served as the last known stronghold of The Order, Elise Bennett and Leo Marquez sat in the dim light of the precinct's evidence room surrounded by boxes of documents, artifacts, and digital media they had seized. Among these items was a cryptic puzzle box that none of the forensics team had been able to open.

"This could be the final piece we need to understand their plans fully," Elise said, her eyes fixed on the intricately carved box on the table between them.

Leo leaned in, his fingers tracing the patterns etched into the wood. "It doesn't seem to have a keyhole or any visible way to open it. Any idea what we're dealing with?"

Elise glanced at the notes they had taken during interviews with captured members of The Order. "One of them mentioned a 'keeper of secrets'— someone responsible for safeguarding The Order's most sacred beliefs. This box could literally be that, holding whatever truths or plans they didn't want to fall into the wrong hands."

As they debated, Dr. Harold Finch, the consultant who had been invaluable in decoding many of The Order's texts, entered the room. "I heard you might have something interesting for me," he said, his gaze settling on the box.

"We believe this might contain critical information about The Order's final intentions," Leo explained, stepping aside to let Finch closer.

Finch examined the box carefully, his experienced eyes picking out details that the detectives hadn't noticed. "These symbols are ancient, Sumerian possibly. See here?" He pointed to a series of marks that looked random to the untrained eye. "These aren't just decorative. They form a sequential lock, a puzzle that needs to be solved in the correct order to open."

"How do we figure out the right sequence?" Elise asked, her mind racing with possibilities.

"It'll require translating these symbols first, then possibly linking them to the lore or rituals that The Order believed in," Finch explained, already pulling out a magnifying glass and a notebook from his bag.

The next hours were spent in deep concentration, with Finch muttering to himself as he worked to translate and make sense of the symbols. Elise and Leo watched, occasionally offering information from the documents they had about The Order's beliefs and practices.

"Here," Finch suddenly exclaimed, his excitement palpable. "Each symbol represents not just an idea, but a specific word that relates to their rituals. For instance, this symbol here stands for 'gateway', and this one for 'knowledge'."

"So, what's the sequence?" Leo leaned in, trying to follow Finch's thought process.

"If my translation is correct, and considering what you've told me about their obsession with celestial alignments, the sequence should reflect their belief in a cosmic order. We start with 'creation', move to 'enlightenment', then 'chaos', and finally 'rebirth'."

Finch carefully pressed the symbols in order, and with a soft click, the box finally opened. Inside, they found a small stack of papers, tightly rolled and bound with a ribbon that had seen better days.

Elise carefully unrolled the first paper, her hands steady despite the adrenaline. The document was a detailed plan for a final ritual, one that intended to 'reset the cosmic balance', according to The Order's belief system. It was scheduled for the upcoming solar eclipse, a date they had thankfully intercepted before it could be carried out.

"This is it," Elise breathed out, relief and resolve mingling in her voice. "This is their endgame. And now we can stop it."

Leo nodded, a serious yet satisfied look on his face. "Let's get this to the team. We'll need every available unit on this. It's not just about catching them anymore—it's about preventing a catastrophe."

As they gathered the papers and secured the box, Elise felt a weight lift off her shoulders. They had the final clue, and with it, the means to end The Order's reign of terror. But the final confrontation was still to come, and they would need to be at their very best to face whatever awaited them.

In the strategic operations room of the precinct, a palpable sense of urgency filled the air as Elise Bennett and Leo Marquez briefed the assembled task force on the impending operation. Maps and digital displays illuminated the room, each showing troop placements and timelines.

"Listen up," Elise began, her voice commanding the attention of everyone present. "Thanks to the breakthrough with the puzzle box, we now have detailed plans for The Order's final ritual. It's set to take place during the solar eclipse, which is less than 48 hours away."

Leo took over, pointing to the digital map. "The location is remote, an old quarry about 40 miles outside of the city. It's secluded, which is why they chose it, but that also works to our advantage. We can approach without being seen."

Detective Gomez, the tactical lead, chimed in. "We've arranged for aerial surveillance starting immediately. Ground units will move in as soon as we have a clear picture of their numbers and defenses."

Elise walked to the front, where the timeline was displayed. "Timing is critical. We need to intercept them before they begin the ritual. Our window is narrow. If they start, it could not only empower them but potentially put us at a disadvantage legally and ethically. We stop this cleanly and by the book."

A younger detective raised a hand. "What's our strategy for the actual approach, Detective Bennett?"

"We'll use a two-tier strategy," Leo responded. "Alpha team will move in first to secure the perimeter and contain the area. Bravo team will then move in to make arrests and secure any materials related to the ritual."

"Remember," Elise interjected, "many of these people may be under the influence of extreme ideological beliefs. Expect resistance but try to minimize confrontation. Use non-lethal force whenever possible."

Detective Harris, responsible for logistics, asked, "How about communication during the op? The quarry is in a dead zone for cell service."

"We've set up mobile repeaters around the quarry to boost signals," Leo explained. "Every team will have radios with multiple channels open, including one directly linked to this command center."

Elise then addressed the group with a firm resolve. "I know we've all been stretched thin, and the pressure is mounting. But we are on the right side of this. We are the barrier between this group and their goal of chaos. Let's bring this to a close."

As the briefing concluded, team members began filing out, moving with purpose and determination. Elise pulled Leo aside for a moment.

"How are you holding up?" she asked, her tone softening.

Leo gave a small, wry smile. "Ready to end this, Elise. Let's just make sure everyone comes home tonight."

"That's the plan," Elise affirmed, clapping him on the shoulder.

They spent the next few hours in the operations room, coordinating with aerial units and making sure every team member knew their role. As the sun began to set, painting the sky with streaks of orange and red, the magnitude of their task seemed to weigh on everyone, a silent acknowledgment of the operation's importance.

By the time they were ready to move out, night had fallen. The task force was a well-oiled machine, each unit moving towards the convoy of vehicles waiting outside.

Elise looked over to Leo as they walked to their vehicle, her expression one of quiet confidence. "Let's finish this."

With a nod, Leo replied, "Tonight, it ends."

As the convoy rolled out, heading towards the quarry, the command center buzzed with activity. Monitors flickered with aerial views and team positions, each movement tracked and logged. The final confrontation with The Order was at hand, and while the outcome was uncertain, the resolve of the task force was clear and unwavering. They were ready to close this chapter, once and for all.

The old quarry, transformed into an eerie estate by The Order, loomed ahead as the task force approached under the cover of darkness. The moonlight cast long shadows across the ground, adding a stark contrast to the glow of tactical lights as the teams moved into position.

Elise Bennett and Leo Marquez led one of the primary entry teams, their movements precise and silent, communicating with hand signals to avoid unnecessary noise. The air was tense, filled with the anticipation of what was about to unfold.

As they neared the perimeter, Elise whispered into her radio, "Alpha team in position on the north side. Bravo, status?"

"Bravo in position on the east approach. Ready on your go," came the response, static crackling briefly in her earpiece.

"Copy that. Hold until we confirm the target location," Elise replied, signaling her team to hold. She turned to Leo, her expression serious under the night-vision goggles. "We need eyes on the ritual site before we make our move. Let's see if we can get a visual without tipping them off."

Leo nodded, and they slowly advanced to a vantage point, a small rise that overlooked the courtyard of the estate where The Order was believed to be gathering. Crouching behind the brush, Elise used a pair of binoculars to survey the area.

"There," she murmured, pointing towards a group of robed figures assembling around what appeared to be a large, ornate setup in the courtyard. "That's got to be the ritual site. Looks like they're just starting to gather."

Leo took a look through the binoculars, confirming her observation. "I see the leader, or at least who appears to be in charge. Matches the description we have of Gregory Hall."

"Okay," Elise said, her mind racing through their options. "We move on my mark. Alpha and Bravo converge on the courtyard. Delta team, you're on extraction and crowd control. Remember, non-lethal force as far as possible."

She relayed the plan over the radio, each team acknowledging their roles. "On my mark... three... two... one... Mark."

With precision, the teams moved in. Elise and Leo led their group directly towards the gathering, the suddenness of their approach causing confusion among The Order's members. Shouts and commands echoed through the night as the tactical teams surrounded the courtyard.

"Police! Everyone down on the ground!" Elise commanded, her voice amplified by the situation's urgency. The members of The Order, though startled, began to comply, some dropping to the ground while others looked around bewildered and scared.

Leo directed some of the officers to secure the leader. "Detain him carefully. Watch for any concealed weapons," he instructed, keeping his eyes on the unfolding scene.

As the initial chaos settled, Elise took a moment to assess the situation. Most of The Order's members were now detained, and her team was methodically searching them and securing the area. She approached one of the robed figures, a middle-aged woman who looked more confused than combative.

"Why are you doing this? Why can't you leave us to our faith?" the woman asked, her voice shaking.

Elise, though empathetic, maintained her professional demeanor. "Your faith has led to harm. We cannot allow that. Anyone hurt or planning to hurt others under the guise of belief poses a danger that we must address."

As the team secured the site and gathered evidence, Leo joined Elise, watching as the detainees were led away. "Looks like we've prevented whatever they were planning tonight," he said quietly.

"Yes, but we need to ensure there's nothing left behind that can reignite this. Let's make sure we gather all documentation and artifacts," Elise responded, her gaze sweeping over the estate.

The operation continued into the early hours, with each officer and detective thorough in their duties. By the time dawn was breaking, the estate was secure, and the immediate threat of The Order's ritual was neutralized, but the work was far from over. The next steps would involve deep investigations into each member and the full extent of the group's intentions and reach. For now, though, Elise and Leo could take a brief moment to acknowledge the night's success—a crucial victory in the ongoing battle against the darkness that had infiltrated their city.

As dawn cast its first light over the quarry turned estate, Elise Bennett and Leo Marquez stood surveying the secured area, with the detained members of The Order now under guard. The tension of the night's operation was giving way to the exhaustion of the long hours, but there was little time for rest; the real confrontation was just beginning.

Gregory Hall, identified as the leader of The Order, had been detained without incident, and now awaited interrogation. Elise and Leo prepared to face him, knowing well that the words exchanged in the next few hours could be crucial in unraveling the full extent of The Order's plans.

In the small, stark interrogation room, Gregory sat calmly, his demeanor collected, almost defiant. As Elise and Leo entered, he looked up, his gaze steady.

"Detective Bennett, Detective Marquez," he began, his voice smooth, betraying no sign of concern. "I suppose I should commend you on disrupting our gathering."

Elise took the seat across from him, her expression unreadable. "Mr. Hall, you're aware of why you're here. This isn't just about a gathering; it's about the actions your group has taken under the guise of religious practice. Actions that have led to harm and chaos."

Gregory smiled thinly. "Ah, but what is chaos but a lack of understanding? Our actions were never meant to harm, but to awaken."

Leo, who had remained standing, interjected sharply. "Your 'awakening' led to deaths, Mr. Hall. That's not enlightenment; it's criminal."

Gregory's smile faded slightly, but his composure remained intact. "Death is but a transition, a mere transformation of states. Those who passed did so by their own belief and conviction."

Elise leaned forward, her tone firm. "That doesn't absolve you of responsibility. You manipulated those beliefs, directed them to serve your purposes. And tonight, we prevented you from taking it even further."

The conversation continued, with Gregory weaving philosophical justifications for every argument, while Elise and Leo countered with the legal and moral implications of his and The Order's actions. Each exchange was a careful dance around laws, beliefs, and the undeniable harm that had been caused.

As the interrogation drew on, Elise knew that breaking Gregory's calm veneer might be impossible. Instead, she focused on extracting as much information as possible about The Order's remaining members and any future plans that might still be lurking in the shadows.

"We have everything we seized last night—documents, artifacts, digital data. It's only a matter of time before we fully expose the breadth of your operations," Elise stated, a subtle warning in her tone.

Gregory's response was a slow nod, the first sign of acknowledgment of his precarious position. "Perhaps, Detective. But ideas cannot be detained, and beliefs will find their soil to grow. What you see as an end, I see as a dispersion."

Leo stood, signaling that the interrogation was over for now. "We'll see how your ideas hold up in court."

As they left the interrogation room, Elise felt a mixture of frustration and achievement. They had stopped a major event, perhaps saved lives, but the ideological battle, the war of beliefs that Gregory spoke of, was far from over.

Back in their makeshift command center, Elise and Leo debriefed with their team, laying out the next steps in the investigation. The morning light brought a new day, but for them, it was just a continuation of the effort to ensure that the seeds of chaos The Order had sown would not take root.

Their drive back to the precinct was quiet, each lost in their thoughts about the complexities of the case and the philosophical underpinnings that made their fight not just against a criminal organization but against a deeply entrenched belief system.

Elise finally broke the silence, her voice thoughtful. "It's not over, Leo. But whatever comes next, we'll face it like we always do—head-on."

Leo nodded, his tired eyes reflecting a steely determination. "Together," he affirmed.

The quarry faded behind them as they drove, the chapter of the night's confrontation closing, but the story of their battle against The Order was still unfolding, the final lines yet to be written.

Chapter 22
Showdown at The Order

The morning was unusually crisp as Detective Elise Bennett and her partner, Detective Leo Marquez, along with a tactical team, approached what they believed to be the final hideout of The Order. Nestled deep in the woods, the secluded house had been under surveillance for weeks, but today, intelligence had confirmed the presence of the last high-value targets inside.

The team moved stealthily through the dense underbrush, communicating with hand signals and the occasional whisper into their radios, coordinating their approach from multiple angles. The house, an old, two-story structure with peeling paint and boarded-up windows, looked less like a bastion of a dangerous cult and more like a forgotten relic of the past.

"Visual on the rear exit," Leo murmured into his radio as he and Elise paused behind a thick grove of trees that offered a clear line of sight to the back door of the house.

"Copy," came the response from the team leader on the other side. "Front team in position. Awaiting your go."

Elise checked her weapon, her focus sharp. "On my mark," she whispered, both to Leo and into her radio. "Three... two... one... Mark."

Simultaneously, the teams converged on the house. The front team breached the main entrance, while Elise and Leo, along with their unit, made their way to the back. The sound of breaking glass and the sudden shouts indicated the front team had made entry.

As they reached the back door, Leo kicked it open, and they swept into the kitchen. The room was empty, but the sound of footsteps above signaled that their targets were aware of the intrusion.

"Clear," Leo called out as they cleared each room on the ground floor, moving methodically and quickly.

"Upstairs," Elise directed, her voice low but urgent. They ascended the stairs, their steps light but fast.

At the top of the stairs, they paused. Elise listened, trying to pinpoint the movements. She gestured to the left. "Two rooms down. I hear movement."

With a nod, Leo followed as they approached the indicated room. Just as they reached the door, it swung open abruptly. A man, his face a mask of fear and determination, lunged out, a makeshift weapon in hand.

Elise reacted instinctively, disarming the man with a swift move taught by years of training. Leo quickly stepped in, securing the suspect with handcuffs.

"Police! You're under arrest!" Elise announced firmly, as the man slumped, defeated.

With one suspect in custody, they cleared the remaining rooms. Each room added to the surreal nature of the day—symbols painted on walls, strange artifacts lining the shelves, and documents strewn about that spoke of the deep-seated beliefs and plans of The Order.

After securing the house and ensuring no other members were inside, Elise stood by a window, looking out at the team as they secured the perimeter. Leo joined her, his expression a mix of relief and contemplation.

"Looks like this might be it, Elise," he said, watching as other officers escorted the cuffed man to one of the vehicles.

Elise nodded, her gaze still fixed on the scene unfolding outside. "It might be, but let's make sure we go through everything here. There might be more to uncover about their operations."

"Agreed," Leo replied. "Let's start with those documents. We need to understand everything they were planning."

As they turned to exit the room, Elise took one last look around, aware of the weight of their discovery. Today marked a significant victory, but the shadows of The Order's influence lingered, a stark reminder of the work still ahead.

They descended the stairs, back into the main part of the house, ready to begin the meticulous process of sifting through the evidence, each step bringing them closer to closing the dark chapter of The Order in their city.

Under the dense canopy of the forest, the evening light waned as Detective Elise Bennett and her team prepared to disrupt what was potentially the final ritual of The Order. Armed with the information gleaned from their recent operations, they knew this could be their last chance to end the group's activities once and for all.

The location, a clearing deep in the woods, had been identified through satellite images and ground reconnaissance as a ritual site. Candles and strange symbols had been arranged in a complex pattern across the forest floor, evident even from the distance.

"Positions, everyone," Elise whispered into her radio as they neared the site. Her team, camouflaged by the underbrush, moved quietly into place, encircling the clearing from all sides.

Leo, positioned next to Elise, peered through his binoculars at the figures robed in dark cloaks, their heads bowed in concentration. "Looks like we're just in time. They haven't started yet."

Elise nodded, her eyes scanning the area for any signs of lookout or additional threats. "We can't let them complete whatever they're planning.

On my signal, we move in. Non-lethal takedowns only, unless absolutely necessary. We need them conscious and capable of standing trial."

As the cult members began to chant, their voices eerie in the twilight, Elise counted down silently. Just as the leader raised his arms, presumably to signal the start of the ritual, she cut her hand through the air, signaling her team.

"Go, go, go!" she commanded, stepping from the cover of the trees with her team following closely behind.

The sudden appearance of law enforcement broke the concentration of the ritual participants. Some tried to flee, scrambling towards the woods, only to be met by officers. Others dropped to the ground, overwhelmed by the swift intervention.

Leo darted forward to apprehend the leader, tackling him just as he reached for something concealed beneath his robe. "You're under arrest," Leo stated firmly, securing the leader's hands behind his back.

Elise moved among the chaos, directing her team and ensuring that all participants were accounted for. "Secure the perimeter! Make sure we have everyone!" she called out.

As the last of the daylight faded, the clearing was bathed in the artificial glow of police flashlights. Officers moved through the area, collecting discarded items that might serve as evidence, including the ritual paraphernalia.

Once all were detained and the site secured, Elise gathered her team for a quick debrief. "Good work, everyone. Let's ensure we document everything before we move out. Photographs, notes, everything needs to be logged."

A junior detective approached Elise with a bag of items. "Detective Bennett, we found these near the altar. Looks like they might have been part of the ritual."

Elise examined the bag briefly, nodding her approval. "Good. Make sure those get tagged and cataloged back at the precinct. They could tell us more about their beliefs and practices."

As the team worked to clear the site, Leo joined Elise, looking around at the now disrupted ritual space. "You think this will be the end of it?"

Elise watched as an officer extinguished the last of the candles. "It's a big step, but something tells me we'll be dealing with the fallout for a while. Ideologies like this don't just disappear. But at least, for now, we've cut them off at the knees."

Leo nodded, his expression somber yet relieved. "Yeah. Let's just make sure we finish the job."

With the ritual disrupted and the participants detained, the team began the meticulous process of evidence collection. Each step was conducted with precision, under the watchful eyes of Elise and Leo, who knew that the successful prosecution of the case depended as much on what happened here as in any courtroom.

The drive back to the precinct was quiet, both detectives contemplating the significance of their actions today. They had prevented something potentially catastrophic, and while the road ahead remained uncertain, tonight they had made a tangible difference.

In the interrogation room back at the precinct, the dim light cast long shadows across the table where the leader of The Order, known as the Puppeteer, sat across from Detectives Elise Bennett and Leo Marquez. Despite his recent capture, the Puppeteer's demeanor remained unnervingly composed, his eyes sharp and calculating.

Elise began the interrogation with a straightforward tone, "You understand why you're here. The ritual was interrupted, but we know there was more planned. What was the end goal?"

The Puppeteer leaned back slightly, a faint smile playing at the corners of his mouth. "Detective, you presume that stopping one ritual stops the essence of what we do. You have merely grasped at the edges of a much larger tapestry."

Leo interjected, his patience thinning. "People were hurt, lives were lost. This isn't just about beliefs or rituals. It's about the law, and you've broken it repeatedly."

"Law is a construct, Detective Marquez, as malleable as the beliefs that govern society," the Puppeteer responded smoothly. "What we offer is transcendence beyond such constructs. Your actions have only delayed the inevitable."

Elise pressed on, trying to break through his philosophical veneer. "Where are the other members? Who else is involved?"

The Puppeteer's gaze did not waver. "The roots of The Order are deeper and more widespread than you can imagine. This is not the end, Detective Bennett. It is an evolution."

Elise took a deep breath, maintaining her composure. "You're looking at serious charges. Cooperation can only benefit you at this point."

A flicker of amusement crossed the Puppeteer's face. "Benefit is also a construct, Detective. I am where I need to be, and The Order will adapt and grow, with or without me."

The room fell silent for a moment, the weight of his defiance hanging in the air. Elise and Leo exchanged a glance, both understanding the gravity of the situation. This was not just a criminal syndicate; it was a belief system that they were trying to dismantle.

Leo stood up, signaling the end of the interrogation for now. "We have enough to keep you here for a long time. Think about your next steps carefully."

As they left the interrogation room, Elise paused outside the door, her mind racing with the implications of the Puppeteer's words. "He's unyielding. We might need another approach to find out how far this network really extends."

Leo nodded, his expression grim. "I'll coordinate with the other departments. See if we can trace any financials or communications that lead out of the city. We need to cut off all the heads of this snake."

The detectives returned to their office, where they began organizing the information gathered from the raid and the subsequent interrogations. Maps dotted with locations connected by lines, financial records sprawled across screens, and photos of artifacts all told a story of a complex and deeply entrenched organization.

Elise focused on piecing together the next steps in their investigation. "We need to keep the pressure on. Search every associated location, freeze assets, and keep a close watch on anyone we've identified as part of this."

Leo worked on a separate terminal, pulling up surveillance footage and cross-referencing faces with known Order members. "I'll also set up round-the-clock monitoring on the high-risk individuals. If anyone makes a move, we'll know about it."

The task was daunting, but Elise and Leo were undeterred. The showdown at the estate had been a significant victory, but the Puppeteer's defiance was a stark reminder of the challenges still ahead. They were ready to face them head-on, armed with the law and a relentless drive to protect the innocent. As they worked late into the night, the precinct buzzed with activity, a beacon of order in the chaos that The Order had tried to unleash.

Back in the interrogation room, Elise Bennett and Leo Marquez faced the Puppeteer once more. The room's stark light cast harsh shadows, mirroring the tension that filled the space. They had returned armed with new evidence and a determination to break through his defiance.

"Let's cut through the philosophy," Elise started, her tone more direct than before. "We've uncovered financial transactions linking you to known criminal organizations, not just spiritual groups. Care to explain that?"

The Puppeteer leaned forward, his hands folded in front of him. "My dear detective, those organizations you mention are merely instruments in a larger symphony. Yes, we sought funds for our cause. The physical plane requires such mundane things, after all."

Leo, who had been reviewing a document, looked up sharply. "You're talking about buying illegal arms, smuggling artifacts, and manipulating vulnerable individuals. This 'symphony' you're conducting has very real victims."

A slight smile flickered across the Puppeteer's face. "You see victims; I see willing participants in a transformative journey."

Elise slammed her hand down on the table, causing the Puppeteer to slightly flinch. "Transformation that ends in death or disappearance is no journey. It's a crime, and you're going to answer for it."

The Puppeteer sighed, the facade of amusement slipping momentarily. "What is life but a series of transformations, Detective? From birth to death, we are constantly changing. I merely expedite that process for those who wish it."

Leo interjected, his voice steely. "And the children? Did they expedite their own transformations when you took them from their homes for your rituals?"

That struck a nerve. The Puppeteer's composed demeanor faltered, his eyes narrowing. "Children are more in tune with the spiritual realities than any adult. We provided them with enlightenment."

"Kidnapping and indoctrination," Elise corrected sharply. "That's what you call enlightenment?"

For a moment, silence hung in the room as the Puppeteer contemplated their accusations. Then, he spoke, his voice softer, but no less convicted. "You are bound by your earthly laws and perceptions. Our laws are universal, eternal. What we offer is beyond your comprehension."

Elise leaned closer, her voice low and intense. "Here's what I comprehend—your 'universal law' ends today. We have everything we need to put you away for life. This is your last chance to lessen that sentence by cooperating."

The Puppeteer met her gaze, a long, calculating look. Finally, he spoke. "Perhaps there is something I can offer..."

Leo quickly interjected, "We're listening, but it better be good."

"I can give you names, locations of other groups, affiliates who operate beyond the reach of your... jurisdiction," the Puppeteer proposed, a trace of resignation in his voice. "In exchange for protection—"

"Protection?" Elise scoffed. "You'll be in custody, but we'll ensure your safety."

With a resigned nod, the Puppeteer finally began to divulge information. Names flowed, locations were listed, and a network began to unfold—a network that extended far beyond what the detectives had initially uncovered.

As the interrogation wrapped up, Elise and Leo stepped outside the room, the weight of the Puppeteer's revelations heavy upon them.

"He gave up more than I expected," Leo noted, his brow furrowed in thought.

Elise nodded, her mind racing with the implications. "It's a big network, Leo. Bigger than we thought. But now we've got a real shot at taking it down."

"We'll need to coordinate with federal and international agencies," Leo said, already thinking ahead to the logistics.

"Let's get to it then," Elise replied, determination lining her features. "We've got a lot of work ahead of us."

As they walked back to their office, the precinct seemed to buzz with a renewed energy. They had cracked open a significant part of the mystery, and while the road ahead was daunting, they were ready to face whatever challenges came next. Tonight, they had struck a significant blow against The Order, and tomorrow, they would begin the task of dismantling it piece by piece.

Chapter 23
Revelation and Confession

The mood was tense in the cold, starkly lit interrogation room of the precinct where Detective Elise Bennett sat across from Marcus Eldridge, one of the key figures in The Order. The dim overhead light cast deep shadows across his face, emphasizing the lines of defiance etched deeply into his visage. Elise, her expression unreadable, was preparing for what she anticipated would be a pivotal confrontation in their ongoing investigation.

Marcus had been brought in under heavy security, his hands cuffed in front of him. Despite his constrained situation, his posture was upright, almost defiant. The room was silent except for the quiet hum of the air conditioning and the faint noise of activity from the precinct outside.

Elise began, her voice steady and authoritative. "Mr. Eldridge, you're aware of why you're here. We've uncovered substantial evidence linking you to numerous illegal activities under the guise of The Order."

Marcus met her gaze, his own eyes unyielding. "Detective Bennett, I've always been forthcoming about my beliefs. My faith in what we do is unshaken. You see it as illegal; I see it as essential."

Elise leaned forward slightly, her tone firm. "This isn't about beliefs, Mr. Eldridge. It's about actions that have led to harm and chaos. You manipulated beliefs to further your own goals, under the protection of what you call 'faith'."

The room fell silent as Marcus considered her words. After a moment, he responded, not with defiance, but with a calculated calmness. "What you call manipulation, I call guidance. People seek meaning, Detective. I provide it."

Elise did not flinch at his justification. "Providing meaning doesn't involve trafficking, harm, or endangering lives. Your 'guidance' led directly to actions that are criminal under the laws of this country."

Marcus smirked slightly, a cold gesture that didn't reach his eyes. "Laws are constructs, Detective. They change. What doesn't change is human nature and its quest for understanding and transcendence."

Elise paused, her strategy clear. She needed to push Marcus to reveal more about the inner workings of The Order, to gain information that could lead to further arrests and dismantling the network. "Your quest has endangered lives, Marcus. It's over. But you have a chance now to reduce the consequences for yourself. Help us understand more, help us prevent further harm."

Marcus leaned back, his eyes narrowing as he considered her offer. After a long moment, he spoke, his voice lower. "What do you want to know?"

Elise's demeanor remained neutral as she took out a list of names and dates. "Let's start with the other members who are still out there. We know you weren't working alone. Who are they? Where can we find them?"

Marcus stared at the paper, his face betraying nothing of his thoughts. Slowly, he began to talk, his words measured, providing names but with little detail.

As the interrogation progressed, Elise took meticulous notes, aware that each piece of information was potentially the key to preventing further plans of The Order. The conversation was laborious, with Marcus providing just enough to keep the dialogue moving but holding back enough to maintain some control.

Outside the interrogation room, Leo Marquez watched through the one-way mirror. He knew that Elise's approach might just break through Marcus's defenses enough to gather essential insights. Each bit of information could lead them deeper into the labyrinth of The Order's operations, closer to understanding the full scope of their agenda.

The confrontation in the interrogation room was just the beginning of a longer, more complex process of unraveling the layers of deception woven by The Order. For Elise, it was a painstaking task, but necessary. Each revelation brought them closer to the truth, and with each truth uncovered, the path to justice became clearer. As Marcus continued to speak, the dim light in the room seemed to grow just a fraction brighter, a metaphor for the gradual illumination of The Order's dark secrets.

The interrogation room had become a stage for the revelations that were slowly unwinding the tightly wound operations of The Order. Detective Elise Bennett, with years of experience in dealing with manipulative criminals, knew that understanding the psyche behind the leader known as the Puppeteer was crucial. Alongside her, Detective Leo Marquez served as a stern but keen observer, understanding that each word from the Puppeteer could lead to significant breakthroughs.

After hours of tactical questioning, they were slowly peeling back the layers of the Puppeteer's motives. His real name, Gregory Hall, had become just a footnote to the infamous title he had earned through his actions.

"Gregory, we know what The Order has done, what you've orchestrated under the guise of spiritual enlightenment. But what I want to understand is why. What drove you to this point?" Elise asked, her tone a mix of curiosity and sternness.

The Puppeteer, who had been leaning back in his chair with an air of detachment, shifted slightly. His eyes, cold and calculating, met Elise's. "Detective, have you never questioned the very fabric of our society? The structures, the rules, the supposed moral compass that guides us?"

Elise kept her expression neutral. "Questioning is one thing. Leading people to their demise is another."

A thin smile crept over the Puppeteer's lips. "Demise, as you call it, is but a transition. My actions were meant to liberate, to ascend beyond the mundane constraints of our flawed society."

Leo interjected, his patience waning. "By causing harm? By breaking families? You call that liberation?"

"It is a small price for the greater good, the evolution of consciousness," the Puppeteer responded, his voice steady and eerily calm.

Elise leaned forward, locking eyes with him. "And the deaths? The families grieving because of your 'greater good'? How do you justify that?"

"There is no evolution without sacrifice. Those who suffered were not victims but participants in a grander plan," the Puppeteer declared, his delusion clear.

Leo and Elise exchanged a quick glance, a silent agreement on the depth of his fanaticism.

"Let's talk about your plans," Elise continued, steering the conversation back to actionable intelligence. "The rituals, the gatherings—what were they all leading to?"

The Puppeteer paused, his demeanor indicating a reluctance to divulge the full extent of his vision. After a moment, he leaned forward. "To an awakening. A societal rebirth. You see chaos and disorder, but I see the birth pangs of a new era."

As the interrogation continued, the detectives gathered crucial details about future plans, locations of hidden documents, and names of key followers who were still at large. Each piece of information was a potential lead to prevent further harm and dismantle the remaining fragments of The Order.

After the session, back in their office, Elise and Leo reflected on the chilling insights they had gained.

"He believes his own rhetoric completely," Elise noted, her voice a mix of astonishment and disgust.

Leo, looking over his notes, added, "True believers are the hardest to dissuade. He's created a narrative that justifies everything, no matter the cost."

As they organized their findings, the task ahead seemed more daunting but clearer. The network was extensive, but the motives were now laid bare, no longer shrouded in the mystical veneer the Puppeteer had crafted around his actions.

"We need to move fast, get ahead of his plans," Elise decided, closing her notebook with a sense of urgency.

Leo nodded in agreement. "We'll set up a task force first thing tomorrow. Sweep every location he mentioned, check every lead."

The day's revelations had provided them with valuable ammunition to continue their fight against The Order's lingering influence. As night fell over the city, the precinct remained a beacon of activity, with every officer and detective driven by the shared goal of preventing the dark vision that the Puppeteer had so fervently believed in from becoming a reality.

Detective Elise Bennett sat in the quiet of her office, the files from The Order spread across her desk like a mosaic of madness and conviction. The lamp cast a warm glow, softening the harsh realities contained within the documents, but it did little to ease the weight on her shoulders.

Leo Marquez knocked softly before entering, his expression somber as he took in the scene. "How are you holding up?" he asked, closing the door behind him.

Elise looked up, managing a tired smile. "It's a lot, Leo. Every piece we uncover, it's like peeling back layers of something much darker and more entrenched than we anticipated."

Leo nodded, pulling up a chair beside her. "I know. But there's something else, isn't there? Something personal about this case for you."

Elise sighed, her gaze falling to a photograph among the files. It showed a younger version of herself alongside another officer, both in uniform, smiling at a police academy graduation. "That's Derek," she said softly. "My brother. He got caught up in a group similar to The Order right out of the academy. We thought it was just a phase, but... he never really came back to us."

Leo's expression softened. "Elise, I had no idea. Is that why—"

"That's why I transferred to this division," Elise interrupted, her voice steady despite the clear pain the memory invoked. "Groups like this, they prey on the vulnerable, on those seeking purpose. Derek was searching for something, and they gave him answers. Dangerous, destructive answers."

Leo reached over, placing his hand over hers. "I'm sorry, Elise. For what it's worth, I think he'd be proud of the work you're doing now."

Elise nodded, pulling her hand back to gather the files. "Maybe. Right now, I just want to make sure no one else goes through what my family did. What Derek did."

The conversation shifted back to the case. "We've got a lead on one of the offshoot groups, based on what the Puppeteer told us," Leo said, changing the subject to something more immediate. "They're meeting tonight, on the outskirts of the city. Thought you might want to be there when we take them down."

Elise looked up, determination flickering in her eyes. "I wouldn't miss it."

Later that evening, as they geared up, Elise felt a familiar mix of adrenaline and resolve. This raid wasn't just part of her job; it was a continuation of her personal crusade against the ideologies that had stolen her brother.

As the team moved out, Leo stayed close. The drive to the location was quiet, each officer lost in their own preparations and thoughts.

Upon arrival, the team quickly and efficiently surrounded the meeting place, an old warehouse that had seen better days. Elise led the entry team, her every sense heightened. As they breached the door, she felt a surge of both professional duty and personal vindication.

The room inside was dimly lit, figures startled as the police stormed in. Commands were shouted, and within minutes, the members were detained, confused and compliant in the face of overwhelming force.

As the suspects were led out, Elise lingered in the warehouse, surveying the scene. Posters, symbols, and paraphernalia that were all too familiar adorned the walls, echoes of the meetings her brother had described in his few communications home.

"Elise?" Leo's voice brought her back to the moment. "We should head back."

"Yeah," she replied, taking one last look around. "Let's go."

As they drove back to the precinct, Elise felt a bittersweet mixture of satisfaction and sorrow. Tonight was a victory, one of many she hoped, but the path to true resolution—both for the city and for herself—was still long and fraught with challenges. But with each raid, each arrest, she was reclaiming a piece of what she had lost. And perhaps, just perhaps, she was finally bringing some peace to her brother's memory.

The precinct was quiet, a stark contrast to the frenetic activity of the last few weeks. Detective Elise Bennett and Detective Leo Marquez sat in the small, somewhat cramped office they shared, surrounded by the remnants of their lengthy investigation into The Order. Files lay open, coffee cups were scattered about, and the whiteboard was covered with names and connections now crossed out or ticked off.

Leo broke the silence, glancing over at Elise who was staring thoughtfully at the board. "It's over, Elise. Or at least, this chapter of it is."

Elise turned to him, her expression weary but relieved. "It feels surreal, Leo. After all this time, to see so many names crossed off... to know that we've actually made a dent."

Leo nodded, understanding her mixed emotions. "It's a big win. You did incredible work."

Elise leaned back in her chair, rubbing her temples. "We did incredible work. Couldn't have done it without you, Leo."

There was a pause, a comfortable silence between the two partners who had weathered the storm together. Then Elise continued, "You know, I kept thinking about Derek through all this. About how things might have been different if someone had intervened sooner... if someone had been there to pull him out."

Leo listened, his expression somber. "You think what we did—stopping The Order—do you think it'll change things?"

Elise sighed, her gaze drifting back to the whiteboard. "I hope so. I have to believe that every person we pulled out of that mess, every ritual we stopped, is a life redirected away from the edge. Maybe it won't change everything, but for those people, it might mean everything."

Leo leaned forward, resting his elbows on his desk. "It's tough, carrying that. Thinking about the 'what ifs'. But you—**you've turned it into something that drives you. Not everyone can do that.**"

Elise smiled faintly, appreciative of his words. "It's not just me, Leo. It's us. It's this team. We might not save everyone, but we save who we can, when we can."

"Speaking of the team," Leo shifted in his chair, pulling his laptop closer. "The chief wants us to prepare a full debriefing. There's going to be a lot of attention on this case now that it's mostly wrapped up."

Elise nodded, her mind already turning to the tasks ahead. "Let's make sure the debrief is thorough. The public, the media, other departments— they'll all want to know how this happened, how it went on for so long, and what we're doing to prevent it in the future."

Leo began typing, organizing their notes and findings into a coherent narrative. "We'll tell them about the warning signs we missed, the lessons we learned. Transparency might make the next case easier to handle, might make people more willing to come forward sooner."

Elise stood, stretching her legs, feeling the weight of the past weeks settling in her bones. "And what about you, Leo? After all this, what's next for you?"

Leo stopped typing, considering her question. "I guess... keep doing this. There are more Orders out there, more people like Derek who might be saved. And as long as there are, I'll keep showing up here."

Elise smiled, her respect for her partner deepening. "Good. Because I was hoping you'd say that. I can't imagine tackling the next one without you."

Leo grinned back at her, closing his laptop with a decisive snap. "Then it's settled. We'll keep showing up. We'll keep fighting."

As they began to gather their materials for the upcoming debrief, the partnership and dedication between them were clear. They were more than just detectives; they were guardians against the darker corners of human belief and behavior, committed to shedding light where there was shadow. The Order's chapter might be closing, but their journey, their fight for justice and protection, was far from over.

Chapter 24
Fall of The Order

The conference room at the city hall was packed with journalists, each eager to cover the downfall of The Order, a story that had gripped the city with its dark undercurrents and dramatic raids. At the front, Detective Elise Bennett and her partner Detective Leo Marquez prepared to address the press, flanked by the Police Chief and the District Attorney.

As the murmur of conversations quieted, the Police Chief took the podium, nodding to the assembled reporters. "Thank you for joining us today. This press conference is to inform the public about the successful dismantling of a group known as The Order, which, as we have discovered, was involved in activities far beyond their publicly stated aims and beliefs."

Elise then stepped up, her presence commanding the room's attention. "Good afternoon. Over the past months, our team has been deeply involved in investigating The Order. What started as an investigation into a series of disturbing incidents and crimes grew into uncovering a widespread network that manipulated, harmed, and exploited its members and others."

A reporter from a major city newspaper raised her hand, her voice cutting through the brief silence that followed Elise's introduction. "Detective Bennett, can you describe the scale of The Order's activities and the impact they had on the community?"

Elise nodded, "The Order had embedded itself deeply within certain communities, presenting itself as a spiritual group. However, our investigations revealed that they were involved in illegal arms dealings, smuggling of artifacts, and serious violations of human rights, including endangering the welfare of children."

Leo added, "To give you an idea of the scale, we executed over thirty raids, with more than fifty arrests, and seized substantial amounts of documents and digital evidence that laid bare the operations of this group."

Another reporter chimed in, "Detective Marquez, were there specific events or tipping points that accelerated the downfall of The Order?"

Leo glanced at Elise before responding, "Yes, there were several key moments. One major breakthrough came from a raid where we disrupted a major ritual gathering that was not just a spiritual event but a cover for planning further illegal activities. The evidence gathered there helped us connect many dots."

Elise continued, "Moreover, our work was significantly aided by community members who came forward with information, tired of the fear and secrecy that surrounded The Order's activities."

A younger journalist in the front row asked, "What measures are being taken to ensure that remnants of this group do not re-form or continue their activities under another guise?"

The District Attorney took this question. "We are working closely with local, state, and federal agencies to monitor any developments. Part of our strategy involves ongoing community outreach to educate the public on the signs of such harmful activities and to strengthen community resistance to such groups."

The room buzzed with the scratch of pens on paper and the soft clicks of cameras as reporters digested the information.

Elise wrapped up her part with a final statement, "This case has been one of the most challenging and complex in our careers. It underscores the need for vigilance and community involvement in policing. The Fall of The Order is not just about law enforcement triumphing; it's about our community reclaiming its safety and integrity."

As the press conference drew to a close, questions continued, each answer shedding more light on the intricate web of deception that had once shrouded The Order. Elise and Leo left the podium, feeling the weight of their public responsibility and the quiet satisfaction of a job well done. This was a significant victory, not just for law enforcement but for the city itself. As they exited into the corridor, the real work of building trust and safety in the wake of such a profound exposure was just beginning.

In the somber confines of the courthouse, Detective Elise Bennett and Detective Leo Marquez sat side by side, their attention focused on the proceedings. The courtroom was filled with the murmur of legal counsel preparing their notes and the subdued shuffling of the audience. The trial of the Puppeteer, the leader of The Order, was about to escalate with the final arguments being presented.

As the district attorney stood, her presence commanded silence. "Ladies and gentlemen of the jury," she began, her voice resonant and clear, "over the course of this trial, we have presented undeniable evidence of the criminal activities conducted under the guise of spiritual enlightenment by the defendant, Gregory Hall, known as the Puppeteer."

Elise whispered to Leo, "She's hitting all the key points. Everything we uncovered is on the table."

Leo nodded, his gaze fixed on the Puppeteer, who sat with an unnervingly calm demeanor. "It's all coming together now. The DA is wrapping it up tight."

The district attorney continued, "Through the testimony of Detective Bennett and Detective Marquez, along with substantial physical evidence, we have shown that this was not merely a group practicing alternative beliefs, but a structured organization engaging in serious criminal conduct, including but not limited to trafficking, illegal arms dealings, and endangering the welfare of minors."

A defense attorney rose for his final statement, attempting to sway the jury with appeals to religious freedom and questioning the interpretation of evidence. "Is it not possible," he posited, looking earnestly at the jury, "that what we see here is a misunderstanding of a spiritual practice? Where is the line drawn between belief and crime?"

Elise muttered under her breath, frustrated, "It's when those beliefs hurt others. That's the line."

Leo leaned slightly towards her, murmuring back, "Don't worry, the jury sees it. The DA made sure of that."

As the defense attorney continued, the district attorney prepared her closing rebuttal, which sharply focused the jury's attention back to the facts. "While freedom of belief is indeed a right, it does not extend to actions that break the law and harm others. The evidence is clear and speaks louder than the philosophical defenses presented."

The judge then addressed the jury, outlining the legal standards and reminding them of their duties. The courtroom's atmosphere thickened with anticipation as the jury retired to deliberate, leaving a palpable silence in their wake.

Elise and Leo stepped outside into the corridor, needing a moment away from the courtroom's stifling tension.

"How do you think it'll go?" Leo asked, watching the jurors' expressions as they had left the room.

Elise considered for a moment before responding. "I think we did everything we could. The evidence is strong, and the DA was compelling. Now, it's up to them to see the truth of it."

They discussed the potential outcomes and implications of the trial, knowing that the verdict would set a significant precedent for how similar cases might be handled in the future.

After what felt like an eternity but was only a few hours, they were called back into the courtroom. The jury filed in, their faces inscrutable, adding to the mounting tension.

As the foreman stood, the room held its breath. "In the case of the State versus Gregory Hall, on the count of conspiracy to commit crime, we find the defendant... guilty."

A wave of relief passed through Elise, her shoulders dropping slightly as the tension ebbed away. Leo placed a reassuring hand on her back, a silent commendation of their hard work.

As the Puppeteer was led away, his stoic façade finally cracked, revealing a flicker of the realization of his new reality.

Outside the courthouse, Elise reflected on the long journey they had undertaken to reach this point. "It's more than just a verdict, Leo. It's a statement—a clear line drawn against using belief to justify harm."

Leo nodded in agreement, "Today, justice did more than just speak; it shouted."

The legal reckoning they had witnessed marked a pivotal moment in their careers and in the lives of those affected by The Order. As they walked down the courthouse steps, the weight of their achievement and the road still ahead was palpable, but so was the sense of a battle well fought and won.

In the aftermath of the successful trial, Detectives Elise Bennett and Leo Marquez convened in the precinct's task force room, now filled with members of the investigative team. The walls, once plastered with photos and string diagrams tracing The Order's activities, were now being cleared, symbolizing the end of a long, arduous case.

Leo looked around the room, addressing the team. "Everyone, this is a significant day for all of us and for the city. The conviction of Gregory Hall marks not just a legal victory but a symbolic end to The Order's reign of manipulation and terror."

Elise nodded, her expression solemn yet relieved. "This was a combined effort. Every officer, analyst, and support staff contributed to this outcome. The dismantling of The Order is a testament to the dedication you all have shown."

A junior detective raised his hand, his expression curious. "What happens now? With Hall convicted, how do we proceed to ensure something like this doesn't happen again?"

Elise leaned forward, her hands clasped in front of her. "Great question. Our work isn't done. We continue to monitor the remnants of the group. We need to stay vigilant and ensure that no offshoots gain traction."

Leo added, "We also expand our community outreach. We learned from this case that community members are invaluable in spotting early signs of similar groups forming. We need to empower and educate the public on what to look out for."

Another detective, who had been heavily involved in the field operations, chimed in. "Do we have any leads on other members who might try to regroup?"

Elise responded, "We've identified several individuals who might pose a risk. We're keeping them under surveillance, and we've got alerts set up if they attempt to contact each other or start new groups."

The room buzzed with further questions and discussions about future strategies and ongoing surveillance operations. The atmosphere was one of cautious optimism—aware of the victory but mindful of the challenges that remained.

A senior analyst, who had been quiet, spoke up. "We've also enhanced our data analytics capabilities. This should help us track and predict patterns that could lead to the formation of similar groups. We're not just reacting now; we're trying to stay a step ahead."

Elise appreciated the proactive approach. "That's excellent. Using technology and data more effectively will definitely make a difference."

As the meeting drew to a close, Leo looked around at the team. "I know it's been a tough few months. Take some time to rest, but let's keep the lines of communication open. We're better prepared now, and we'll handle things differently going forward."

The team began to disperse, with some staying behind to discuss specific details or to update the databases with the latest information.

Elise and Leo took a moment to themselves, reflecting on the journey.

Leo sighed, a mix of fatigue and satisfaction in his voice. "You know, Elise, when we started this, I wasn't sure we'd see the end of it."

Elise smiled, looking at the now almost-empty walls. "I had my doubts too. But here we are. It's more than just the fall of The Order. It's about setting a precedent."

Leo nodded, "Exactly. And protecting the next potential Derek," he added, acknowledging Elise's personal stake in the case.

Elise's smile faded into a more serious expression. "Yes, protecting them all. Let's keep pushing, Leo. There's more out there, and they need us."

As they left the task force room, the light fading outside marked the end of the day but also symbolized the beginning of a new phase of vigilance and prevention. The demise of The Order was a chapter closed, but the story of their fight against such threats was far from over. The lessons learned and the strategies developed from this case would now bolster their efforts in safeguarding the community against future dangers, each step forward driven by the commitment and resolve shown in the takedown of The Order.

As the sun set over the city, casting long shadows between the buildings, Detectives Elise Bennett and Leo Marquez found themselves at a small, quiet cafe, a stark contrast to the bustling energy of the precinct. With the case officially closed, this was their first moment in weeks to sit and truly reflect without the pressure of immediate tasks.

Elise stirred her coffee slowly, her gaze fixed on the swirl of cream blending into the dark liquid. "You know, Leo, today at the debrief, when I saw all those files being archived, it felt surreal. Like closing a book I wasn't sure had an ending."

Leo nodded, taking a sip of his coffee. "It's been a long road. I keep thinking about all those people we talked to, how deep this went. It's more than just putting away the bad guys."

Elise smiled faintly. "Yeah, it's about the impact, the change. I think about my brother, Derek. This started as a way to understand what happened to him, maybe to make sure it didn't happen to anyone else."

Leo leaned back, his eyes thoughtful. "Do you feel like we've done that? Made it right?"

Elise paused, considering. "I think we've done what we could. It's not just about making it right, but about learning and making sure we're better prepared next time. We've set something in motion, a good thing. And that counts for a lot."

Leo chuckled softly. "You always were the optimist between us. But you're right. We've sparked a change. And that's what matters."

Their conversation drifted to the lighter topics, a brief respite from their usual intense discussions about cases and leads. But soon, the conversation turned back to the weightier issues at hand.

"You think there'll be another Order? Another group like this?" Leo asked, his tone serious again.

Elise set down her coffee cup, her expression sober. "There might be. But we're better now, smarter and more connected to the community. We've learned a lot, and that knowledge is our best defense."

Leo nodded. "And we've got each other's backs. That's got to count for something."

Elise looked at Leo, her eyes conveying gratitude. "It counts for a lot, Leo. I couldn't have asked for a better partner through all this."

The conversation slowed as they both took a moment to enjoy the quiet around them, a luxury that had been scarce during the investigation.

Leo broke the silence, a slight grin appearing. "So, what's next for Detective Bennett? Taking a long vacation, I hope?"

Elise laughed, shaking her head. "Maybe a short one. But then it's back to work. There are more cases, more people who need help. And someone's got to be there to do it."

Leo raised his coffee cup in a small toast. "To being there. Today, tomorrow, and as long as it takes."

Elise clinked her cup against his. "To being there."

As they finished their coffees and prepared to leave, the weight of their experiences hung between them, a shared bond forged in the trials they had faced together. They stepped out of the cafe into the cooling evening, the city sounds a backdrop to their quiet companionship.

Walking back to their cars, the partnership they shared was a testament to their commitment, not just to their badges but to the city and its people. The fall of The Order was a chapter closed, but the story of their service, their dedication to justice, and their care for the community would continue, each step forward a reflection of the lessons learned and the closure they had fought so hard to achieve.

Chapter 25
New Beginnings

As the city embraced the shift towards normalcy after the tumultuous fall of The Order, Detective Elise Bennett found herself walking the quiet paths of the city's oldest park. The serene environment, with its ancient oaks and tranquil pond, offered a stark contrast to the chaos that had recently consumed her days. The calmness of nature provided not just a respite but a necessary space for reflection and healing.

Elise's thoughts wandered back to the many victims affected by The Order's deceit. Families broken apart, lives irrevocably altered. It was now a time for rebuilding, for the community and for those directly touched by the darkness of the cult. As part of the healing process, the police department, under her initiative, had set up community outreach programs designed to support these victims, providing counseling services and legal assistance to help them reclaim their lives.

Meanwhile, across town in a bustling community center, Leo Marquez was involved in a different kind of rebuilding. He was leading a workshop aimed at educating the public about the signs of harmful groups and the importance of community vigilance. The room was filled with attentive faces, each participant eager to learn and understand more about protecting themselves and their loved ones.

"Understanding the signs of manipulation and control is crucial," Leo explained, his voice echoing slightly in the filled room. "It's not just about avoiding these groups but also about knowing how to help others who might be entangled in similar situations."

His words were met with nods of agreement and the scribbling of notes. The community's engagement was a positive sign, a reflection of their collective desire to move forward and prevent future tragedies.

Back in the park, Elise sat on a bench by the pond, watching a pair of ducks glide across the water. Her thoughts shifted to her brother, Derek. The case had brought them unexpectedly closer, bridging gaps widened by years and misunderstandings. Derek was now undergoing therapy, dealing with the remnants of his time with The Order. Their conversations, once strained, had become more frequent and filled with hope.

This personal healing was mirrored in the broader community efforts. Support groups had sprung up, facilitated by local charities and backed by police liaisons, providing a forum for ex-members and affected families to share their experiences and support each other. Elise often attended these meetings, not just as a detective but as someone personally touched by the group's influence. Her presence and personal story lent a deeper credibility to the efforts, bridging the gap between law enforcement and the community.

As the afternoon waned, Elise stood and continued her walk, her steps slow and thoughtful. The path wound through a newly planted area of the park, where each tree represented a victim of The Order. A small plaque at the entrance of this memorial grove explained its significance, a testament to both loss and resilience.

The tranquility of the park and the proactive energy of the community center were just two aspects of the city's healing process. Both spaces, though different in nature, were vital to the communal and individual healing journeys.

As Elise left the park, the setting sun cast long shadows on the path ahead. The road to recovery was just beginning, and while the challenges were many, the collective spirit of the community promised a future where such darkness would find it much harder to take root. The time for healing was now, and as the city healed, so too did its inhabitants, drawing strength from their shared experiences and from the support that now thrived in previously broken places.

In the early hours of the morning, before the city fully awoke, Detective Leo Marquez was already at his desk, pouring over files and community feedback forms. His recent workshops had sparked a new initiative within the department—developing a comprehensive program that aimed not only at prevention but also at aiding recovery for those affected by groups like The Order.

Detective Sandra Chen, Leo's colleague, joined him, her eyes scanning the cluttered surface of his desk. "You're here early," she remarked, setting down a cup of coffee for him, which he accepted with a grateful nod.

"Yeah, I've been thinking about how we can better integrate our efforts with other organizations—make sure we're not just reacting but really making a difference," Leo explained, gesturing towards the stack of forms. "There's a lot of good feedback here, and some serious gaps in our outreach that we need to address."

Sandra, who had been deeply involved in some of the field operations against The Order, nodded in understanding. "I saw that. The community trusts us more now; they're really starting to open up. It's a big opportunity for us to step up our game."

Leo sipped his coffee, his mind racing with ideas. "Exactly. I'm planning to propose a new unit, one that focuses on prevention through education and active community engagement. Not just workshops but ongoing support, regular check-ins, and resources that are easily accessible."

"That sounds like a significant commitment," Sandra commented, pulling up a chair. "Do you think the brass will go for it?"

"I think they will. After everything that's happened, they know we can't just go back to business as usual. We need a dedicated team, and I'm ready to lead it if they'll let me," Leo stated, his determination clear.

The conversation was interrupted by a phone call from Elise, checking in before her meeting with the mayor about community rehabilitation projects. Leo updated her on his plans, and her response was immediately supportive.

"That's a fantastic initiative, Leo. It's exactly what we need right now. Let me know if you need me to back you up with the command staff," Elise offered, her voice energetic even through the phone.

"Thanks, Elise. I might take you up on that," Leo replied, a smile breaking through his usually serious demeanor.

After hanging up, Leo and Sandra discussed potential strategies for the new unit, considering everything from staffing and funding to potential partnerships with local schools and psychological services. The scope of their planning reflected Leo's ambition not just to prevent future groups like The Order from forming, but also to heal the community's existing wounds.

Sandra, while supportive, raised practical concerns. "We're going to need solid metrics for success. It can't just be about feelings; we need to show real, quantifiable progress."

"You're right," Leo acknowledged. "We'll set up a system for tracking engagement and outcomes. Maybe partner with a local university for data analysis. Show that what we're doing isn't just feel-good but effective."

As the morning light began to fill the office, the plans on Leo's desk evolved from ideas to a drafted proposal. His commitment to making a lasting change was evident in every line of the document, each word carefully chosen to convey the importance and necessity of the initiative.

Finishing his coffee, Leo stood up, stretching slightly. "I think we've got a strong case here, Sandra. Let's polish this and get it ready for presentation."

Sandra stood as well, gathering the forms and notes. "Let's do it. This could change the way we handle things moving forward—a real legacy of the work we've done."

As they left the office to prepare for a series of meetings that would determine the fate of the proposal, Leo's resolve was clear. This new chapter was not just about moving on from the past but about learning from it and using those lessons to create a safer, more engaged community. His continued commitment was a beacon of progress, signaling a new era not just for the precinct, but for the entire city.

On a bright, clear day, the community gathered in a local park, now revitalized as a symbol of recovery and remembrance. A new monument stood at the center, dedicated to those affected by The Order. The ceremony was not just a commemoration but also a celebration of new beginnings, and Detective Elise Bennett was among the key speakers.

As the crowd settled, Elise took the podium, her notes prepared but her heart leading her words. "Today, we stand together not just to remember the past but to mark a path forward," she began, her voice clear and resonant. "This monument is dedicated to the resilience of those who endured, to the community that supported them, and to the ongoing commitment of those who work to ensure such darkness does not take hold again."

The audience, a mix of citizens, law enforcement officials, and local leaders, listened intently. Among them was Leo Marquez, who watched Elise with a sense of pride and accomplishment.

After the ceremony, Leo joined Elise as they walked through the park. "You were great up there," he said, gesturing towards the podium now being cleared.

Elise smiled, looking around at the families enjoying the renovated space. "It feels good to put a positive stamp on all this, doesn't it? To celebrate not just the end of The Order but the strength it brought out in our community."

Leo nodded, his eyes scanning the new playgrounds and walking paths. "It does. And seeing all this—kids playing, people talking—it's a real change from where we started."

Their conversation was interrupted by Mayor Hernandez, who approached with a grateful smile. "Detective Bennett, Detective Marquez, I can't thank you enough for today, and for all your work. This park, this event—it's a real turning point for us."

Elise acknowledged the mayor's words. "Thank you, Mayor. It's important for us, too. Being able to see a tangible result of our efforts, it helps. It's not just about catching the bad guys; it's about helping the community heal."

The mayor looked around, his expression thoughtful. "And heal we will. I'm committed to supporting your new initiatives, Leo. The council is fully behind your community engagement program. We see it as essential to our city's future."

Leo responded warmly, "That's great to hear, Mayor. We're ready to get started. We believe it can make a real difference."

As the afternoon wore on, Elise and Leo continued to mingle with the attendees, each conversation reinforcing the community's support and appreciation for their efforts. Parents thanked them, local business owners offered support for future police initiatives, and children played around the monument, a lively symbol of the community's resurgence.

Towards the end of the event, Elise and Leo found a moment to reflect by the monument, which was engraved with names and messages of hope and renewal.

Leo glanced at Elise, a reflective look on his face. "You ever think about how all this started? That first day we got the case?"

Elise laughed softly, "Every day. It's been a journey, hasn't it? From uncertainty to today... it's more than I could have hoped for."

Leo placed his hand on the monument, tracing the engravings. "It's a legacy, Elise. Something that'll outlast us and remind everyone what we're capable of when we come together."

Elise joined him, her hand next to his. "A legacy of light out of darkness. Let's keep that light burning, Leo. For Derek, for the community, for everyone who needs it."

As they stood in quiet solidarity, the setting sun cast a golden glow over the park, the light playing over the names on the monument. The legacy of their work, encapsulated in this place of peace and remembrance, was a testament to their dedication and a beacon for the future. The event closed with a sense of collective accomplishment and hope, the community united in its desire to continue building on the foundation of resilience and renewal that had been so hard-won.

The setting sun cast a warm glow over the city as Detectives Elise Bennett and Leo Marquez walked down the bustling streets lined with early evening shoppers and diners. They had just left a community outreach meeting, feeling optimistic about the new initiatives set to roll out across the city.

Elise looked over at Leo, a small smile playing on her lips. "You know, I never thought I'd see the day when our work would start to feel... well, somewhat normal again. Like we're actually making a difference not just in the immediate, but in the big picture too."

Leo chuckled, his eyes reflecting the golden hour light. "I know what you mean. It's like we're finally steering the ship in the right direction after being in rough seas for so long."

Their conversation continued as they stopped at a street vendor, Leo buying them both a cup of coffee. As they walked, sipping their drinks, Leo said, "These community meetings have been eye-opening. People really do appreciate the efforts we're making. And that feedback about the neighborhood patrols was pretty encouraging."

Elise nodded, taking a sip of her coffee. "Absolutely. And it's not just about being seen. It's about being approachable, about making sure people feel they can come to us with anything. That kind of trust... it's hard won but so worth it."

As they turned a corner, they passed by a new community center that had opened as part of the revitalization efforts. "See that?" Elise pointed. "Two months ago, that was just another rundown building. Now, it's a place where kids go after school, where job fairs are held, and where support groups meet. It's tangible change."

Leo's expression turned thoughtful. "It's good. But we've got to keep the momentum going. Not just pat ourselves on the back and call it a day. The real work, the sustaining work, that starts now."

Elise agreed, her tone serious. "I've been thinking about that. About how we ensure this isn't just a flash in the pan. We've seen too many programs start strong and then fizzle out."

"That's why I'm pushing for that ongoing funding proposal," Leo responded, his gaze firm. "We need to make sure there's a steady stream, not just grants that dry up. If we can secure that, we can plan long-term, make sure these programs don't just survive but thrive."

Elise stopped walking, looking at Leo with a renewed sense of respect. "I'm glad you're on top of that. I've been so wrapped up in the outreach itself, I haven't thought as much about the logistics as I should."

Leo smiled, nudging her playfully. "Hey, that's why we're a team, right? You keep us focused on the ground, I'll handle the numbers and the boring paperwork."

They resumed walking, the city sounds blending with their light laughter. As they neared the precinct, Elise's tone grew more contemplative. "Leo, do you ever think about what's next? I mean, personally, after all this?"

Leo looked at her, his expression softening. "Sometimes, yeah. I think about teaching more, maybe at the academy. Sharing what we've learned here, not just about policing but about community, about resilience."

"And you'd be great at that," Elise affirmed. "As for me, I think I'm right where I need to be. Maybe someday I'll look to do something else, but for now, there's too much good we can still do here."

They reached the precinct, their steps slowing as they approached the entrance. Leo held the door open for Elise, a gesture familiar and filled with camaraderie.

"Tomorrow's another day, Elise. Another step forward," Leo said as they entered the building.

"Another step forward," Elise repeated, her voice a mixture of determination and hope. They stepped into the precinct together, ready to face whatever challenges awaited, supported by the foundation they had built in their relentless pursuit of a safer, stronger community.

Conclusion

As the city of Veridian finally settled into a semblance of normalcy, Detective Elise Bennett and her partner, Leo Marquez, found themselves reflecting on the intricate web of crime and conspiracy they had untangled. The once elusive Puppeteer and his nefarious Order had been exposed, their plans thwarted through the tireless efforts of the detectives and their team. Now, with the trials concluded and justice served, the broader implications of their investigations began to ripple through the community.

In a quiet room within the precinct, Elise and Leo pored over their case notes, the files now closed but the memories vivid. "You know, all these months, we chased shadows," Elise mused, closing a folder. "I can't help but think about the lives we've impacted. Not just the victims, but those who were on the edge of this whole mess without even knowing it."

Leo nodded, understanding her sentiment. "It's the ripple effect. But we did good, Elise. Think about the families that won't have to go through what the victims did because we stopped it from going any further."

Their conversation was interrupted by Captain Emilio Sandoval, who entered with a small smile. "I just wanted to say good work, you two. The city owes you more than it can ever pay back. With this case, you've set a new standard for all of us here."

As the winter gave way to spring, the city held a small ceremony in the park. It was not just to commend the police force, but also to heal as a community. People from all walks of life—those who had been touched by the darkness of The Order and those who had merely watched the events unfold—gathered under the budding trees.

Elise and Leo stood together, a bit apart from the festivities, watching families enjoy the peace of a normal day. "It feels like an end, doesn't it?

An end to a chapter, at least," Leo remarked, hands in his pockets, looking out at the crowd.

"More like a new beginning," Elise corrected softly, a hopeful undertone in her voice. "For all of us. This case... it took a lot out of us, but look at what it's brought. Awareness, caution, and maybe a bit more understanding of the depths to which the human mind can sink, but also how resilient it can be."

Leo smiled at her, the weight of months lifting in the light of her optimism. "So, what's next for you, Bennett? Another dark corner of Veridian to shine your light into?"

Elise laughed lightly, the sound mingling with the murmur of the park. "Wherever I'm needed. Wherever we're needed," she corrected, nudging him lightly with her elbow. "Partners, remember?"

"Always," Leo agreed, his gaze following a couple of kids chasing each other around a nearby fountain.

As the ceremony drew to a close, the mayor dedicated a new plaque in the park, commemorating not only those who had fallen but celebrating the resilience of the community and the protectors who stood watch over it. Elise and Leo joined the applause, their claps echoing the renewed spirit of Veridian.

Walking back to their cars, the partners knew that the end of this case didn't mean a stop to their work. There were always more mysteries to solve, more shadows to chase. But today, they took a moment to just breathe, to recognize their victory not just for themselves, but for their city.

Elise glanced over at Leo, a smirk playing on her lips. "Ready to start the next chapter?"

"After a good night's rest," Leo replied, his laughter mingling with hers as they stepped into the evening, ready for whatever lay ahead.